THE SKIN I'M IN

CORETTA SCOTT KING AWARD WINNER

"When Sharon G. Flake's *The Skin I'm In* was originally published in 1998, it was a game-changer that sparked an urgent dialogue about race. This is a fearless, inspirational, groundbreaking novel. It now stands among the pantheon of contemporary classics that is embraced by anyone who cares deeply about opening the minds and hearts of teenagers. **Maleeka Madison's story is as relevant and as necessary today as it was two decades ago.** Mothers, sisters, aunts, and girlfriends of every complexion are passing down this singular book to the young women in their lives, showing them that what they see in the mirror is, without question, beautiful."

—ANDREA DAVIS PINKNEY, publisher and editor of *The Skin I'm In*, and *New York Times* best-selling author of *The Red Pencil*

"I remember sneaking *The Skin I'm In* out of my classroom library again and again as a middle schooler; I barely let any of the other kids read it. Then I was drawn to how honest Flake's language felt, how unflinchingly she told a story to which I could relate. Reading it twenty years later, I realize Flake's story still has its ear to the heartbeat of a young person who is trying to become her own hero while facing the cruelty of her peers. This is **a narrative that shows the complexity of colorism, poverty, self-hate, and girlhood.** This book was moving when I was twelve and needed to cement my inner strength, and it is still just as moving now."

—ELIZABETH ACEVEDO, *New York Times* best-selling author of *Beastgirl and Other Origin Myths* and *The Poet X*

THE SKIN I'M IN

SHARON G. FLAKE

FOREWORD BY JASON REYNOLDS

LITTLE, BROWN AND COMPANY
New York   Boston

Also by Sharon G. Flake

Bang!
Who Am I Without Him?
You Don't Even Know Me
Money Hungry
Begging for Change

Little, Brown and Company
Hachette Book Group
1290 Avenue of the Americas, New York, NY 10104
Visit us at LBYR.com

Originally published in hardcover by Disney • Jump at the Sun, an imprint of Disney Book Group, in October 1998
Twentieth Anniversary Edition: October 2018

Little, Brown and Company is a division of Hachette Book Group, Inc. The Little, Brown name and logo are trademarks of Hachette Book Group, Inc.

The publisher is not responsible for websites (or their content) that are not owned by the publisher.

Library of Congress Control Number: 98019615

ISBNs: 978-1-368-01943-9 (pbk.), 978-1-423-13251-6 (ebook)

Printed in the United States of America

CC

10 9 8 7 6 5 4

FOREWORD BY JASON REYNOLDS

There are gifts we give to mark moments. Gifts that come with meaning attached. Sometimes they come in the form of a piece of jewelry—a gold chain, a special ring, a new charm for an old bracelet. Or an heirloom left behind by a lost loved one. For me, these milestone markers are books, and none have been given more often than Sharon Flake's *The Skin I'm In.*

I come from a family of women. My mother, one of three sisters, was the only one to have sons. Everyone else, including my older sister, had daughters. There came a natural (though complex) window where it seemed as though all the young ladies in my family—my little cousins, goddaughters, nieces—were all approaching puberty around the same time. These little girls, plaits and ponytails, crooked smiles, wrapped in beautiful brown skin, suddenly all seemed to walk with heavy feet, with rolled shoulders. They seemed to mouse their voices, tamp a familiar moxie, and fold into themselves in ways that felt like they were trying to hide.

But who were they hiding from?

This was always the question I asked, the question they would never answer, and that I, in fear of overstepping, left alone. But while working in a bookstore at nineteen, I came across this novel. The cover a tight shot of a black girl with glossy ebony skin. I read it in one sitting while manning the register, and realized this gem was going to be given to every young girl in my family. I would make it their Christmas presents, that way it would be less heavy-handed, less intrusive. Because there's nothing a young girl hates more than her older male cousin telling her how to feel. And for good reason.

Thankfully, now these girls had Maleeka.

She gave them a place to put their secrets. Gave them a homegirl to lean on. She told them it was okay to be who they were, to look how they looked, to feel how they felt. Maleeka was a reminder that not only were their experiences valid, their existence was valuable.

As much as my cousins, goddaughters, and nieces needed this book fifteen years ago, it may be even more necessary now. With social media becoming a primary form of communication (or miscommunication), young people have never compared themselves to other people more than they do today. They've never scrutinized what others see as flaws, or had to combat phantom bullies as they do now. And the internet isn't going anywhere. Social media isn't going anywhere. So we're fortunate—extremely fortunate—that *The Skin I'm In* is also here to stay. Before incredible movements and monikers like Black Girls Rock, Black Girl Magic, and Well-Read Black Girl, there was *The Skin I'm In*, which is not just a book, but a platform for young people—especially the Maleekas of the world—to stand on, chin up, shoulders back, voices lifted, beaming.

THE SKIN
I'M IN

CHAPTER ONE

THE FIRST TIME I SEEN HER, I got a bad feeling inside. Not like I was in danger or nothing. Just like she was somebody I should stay clear of. To tell the truth, she was a freak like me. The kind of person folks can't help but tease. That's bad if you're a kid like me. It's worse for a new teacher like her.

Miss Saunders is as different as they come. First off, she got a man's name, Michael. Now who ever heard of a woman named that? She's tall and fat like nobody's business, and she's got the smallest feet I ever seen. Worse yet, she's got a giant white stain spread halfway across her face like somebody tossed acid on it or something.

I try not to stare the first day that amazon woman-teacher heads my way. See, I got a way of attracting strange characters. They draw to me like someone stuck a note on my forehead saying, "losers wanted here." Well, I spend a lot of time trying to fit in here at McClenton Middle School. I ain't letting nobody ruin it for me, especially no teacher.

I didn't even look up when Miss Saunders came up to me that day like I'm some kind of information center.

"Excuse me," she says. She's wearing a dark purple suit, and a starched white shirt with matching purple buttons. That outfit costs three hundred dollars, easy. "I'm trying to find the principal's office. I know it's around here somewhere. Can you help me?"

Before I catch myself, my eyes ricochet like pin balls, bounding from John-John McIntyre's beady brown eyes right up to hers. I swallow hard. Stare at her till John-John whacks me on the arm with his rolled-up comic book.

"That-a-way," I say, pointing up the hall.

"Thank you. Now what's your name?" she says, putting down her briefcase like she's gonna stay here awhile.

"Maleeka. Maleeka Madison—the third," I say, smacking my gum real loud.

"Don't let that fancy name fool you," John-John butts in. "She ain't nobody worth knowing."

Miss Saunders stares down at him till he turns his head away and starts playing with the buttons on his shirt like some two-year-old.

"Like I say, the office is that-a-way." I point.

"Thank you," she says, walking off. Then she stops stone still, like some bright idea has just come to her, turns around, and heads back my way. My skin starts to crawl before she even opens her mouth. "Maleeka, your skin is pretty. Like a blue-black sky after it's rained and rained," she says. Then she smiles and explains how that line comes from a favorite poem of hers. Next thing I know, she's heading down the hall again like nothing much happened.

When she's far enough away, John-John says to me, "I don't see no pretty, just a whole lotta black." Before I can punch him good, he's singing a rap song. "Maleeka, Maleeka—baboom, boom, boom, we sure wanna keep her, baboom, boom, boom, but she so black, baboom, boom, boom, we just can't see her."

Before I know it, three more boys is pointing at me and singing that song, too. Me, I'm wishing the building will collapse on top of me.

John-John McIntyre is the smallest seventh grader in the world. Even fifth graders can see over his head. Sometimes I have a hard time believing he and me are both thirteen. He's my color, but since second grade *he's* been teasing *me* about being too black. Last year, when I thought things couldn't get no worse, he came up with this here song. Now, here this woman comes talking that black stuff. Stirring him up again.

Seems like people been teasing me all my life. If it ain't about my color, it's my clothes. Momma makes them by hand. They look it, too—lopsided pockets, stitching forever unraveling. I never know when a collar's gonna fall off, or a pushpin gonna stick me and make me holler out in class. I stopped worrying about that this year now that Charlese lends me clothes to wear. I stash them in the locker and change into them before first period. I'm like Superman when I get Charlese's clothes on. I got a new attitude, and my teachers sure don't like it none.

It's bad enough that I'm the darkest, worst-dressed thing in school. I'm also the tallest, skinniest thing you ever seen. And people like John-John remind me of it every chance they get. They don't say nothing about the fact that I'm a math whiz, and can outdo ninth graders when it comes to figuring numbers. Or that I got a good memory and never forget one single, solitary thing I read. They only see what they see, and they don't seem to like what they see much.

Up till now, I just took it. The name calling. The pushing and shoving and cheating off me. Then last week something happened. I was walking down the hall in one of Char's dresses, strutting my stuff, looking good. Then

Char walked up to me and told me to take off her clothes. There was maybe eight or nine kids around when she said it, too, including Caleb. I thought she was kidding. She wasn't. So I went to the girls' room and put my own stuff back on. That's when I made up my mind. Enough is enough. I deserve better than for people to treat me any old way they want. But saying that is one thing, making it happen is something else.

So you see, I got my own troubles. I don't need no scar-faced teacher making things worse. But I got this feeling Miss Saunders is gonna mess things up for me real bad.

CHAPTER TWO

JOHN-JOHN THINKS HE SMART. I hear him still singing that boom-boom song under his breath. I don't have to listen to it, either. So instead of going to fifth period and sitting next to him, I'm going outside. There's plenty of kids hanging out around the corner at the pretzel place. I just have to get to my locker for my coat and slip out the backdoor. Soon as I get down the hall, though, who do I see but that woman. She's all up in somebody else's business already.

"Young lady," she says to a girl leaning against the wall with a boy sucking on her neck. "Get to class."

I turn to a locker like I'm trying to open it. When the girl turns Miss Saunders's way, I almost choke on my spit. It's Charlese. Man, the stuff's gonna fly now. Charlese stares at Miss Saunders like she's out of her mind. Then

6

she laughs. I see Miss Saunders, crunching up her face, and cutting her eyes at Worm.

Worm busts out laughing and says, "Dang, who you? Somebody's momma?"

"I'm the new English teacher." Miss Saunders has got a real attitude when she says it, too.

"Shoot," Char says. "I sure ain't looking at that face forty-five minutes every day. No way."

Worm puts his arm round Char's shoulder. They walk down the hall right past me. "Dang. What happened to her?" he whispers. They head for the stairway to keep on locking lips.

"To class or to the office," Miss Saunders calls after them real loud and steady.

Charlese looks at Miss Saunders and rolls her eyes.

Miss Saunders has got her hands on her hips. "You have something to say?"

Big mistake, lady, I'm thinking. Charlese is the baddest thing in this school. She ain't gonna forgive you for loud-talking to her.

Charlese, she's crazylike. Next thing I know, she's telling Miss Saunders to mind her own business. She says something about her face. Worm's telling Char to cool it. He's dragging her down the hall with his hand covering her big mouth. The new teacher don't know when to quit. She tells Worm to hold on a minute. Then she says her piece. She's letting Charlese know that she's traveled all over the world, and there's nothing Charlese can say about her face that she ain't heard in at least four different languages.

Char says, "If you're so high and mighty, what're you doing in a dump like this?"

Miss Saunders puts down her briefcase. When she does, her Gucci watch flashes. This lady's got money. Big-time cash.

"I want to give something back," Miss Saunders says.

"You want to give something back?" Charlese asks, putting out her hand. "Good. You can start by giving me them designer shoes and that three-hundred-dollar watch you got on."

Charlese, she's got an eye for the good stuff. Her older sister JuJu, who's been taking care of Char since their parents died two years back, has got all kinds of stuff at her house. Most of it still got price tags on it. She'll sell you a three-hundred-dollar pants suit for fifty dollars, or a nice coat for a Benjamin—a hundred bucks. Good deals if you got the dollars, which I ain't. Char's lucky. When my daddy died three years ago, Momma took to her sewing machine to help her ease the pain. I sure wish she'd taken to getting me clothes off a store rack, instead. Her sewing is a shame.

Worm tells Charlese to forget about Miss Saunders and to get outta here. Charlese don't let the new broad off so easy.

"You don't scare me," she says, putting her hands on her hips, but before Miss Saunders can speak, here comes Tai, interrupting everything.

"I see you've met Charlese," Tai says to Miss Saunders.

Tai teaches math. She is weird, too. She stands at the blackboard with one leg leaning on the other like a flamingo. She does yoga and hums like a heater on the blink. Tai is a strange chick, I'm telling you.

"I see you made it," she says to Miss Saunders, grabbing both her arms and squeezing them tight in a friendly girl-to-girl squeeze.

Tai looks funny standing next to Miss Saunders, who must be close to six feet tall. Tai is short with long hair and two sets of silver hoop earrings in her ears, and a small hole in her nose where she puts her nose ring when she ain't at work.

"We're old college roommates," she says to Charlese. "You will love having this woman around. She really makes things happen."

I don't know why Tai is telling all this to Charlese. She

knows Charlese couldn't care less. Tai and Miss Saunders head for the office. Tai tells Worm and Charlese to get to class.

"Sure, Tai," Char says, all sweet and innocent.

When Char is halfway up the hall, Tai looks over her shoulder at me and says, "That goes for you, too, Miss Madison."

CHAPTER THREE

WE'RE IN THE GIRLS' ROOM—like always. For once, I'm really trying to pee, not just talk about folk. That's hard in this school. Ain't no doors on the stalls. The principal took them off himself, so everything we do is out in the open. Like that's gonna stop girls from smoking cigarettes, writing on the walls, and cutting class.

Everybody's talking about the new teacher. "Her face looks like somebody threw a hot pot of something on it," Char says, frowning. "If I had a mug like that, I'd kill myself," she says, lifting up her arms and smelling her pits. I want to tell her that if I had hair balls as big as basketballs growing under my arms like she does, *I'd* kill *myself.* But I don't say what's on my mind. I keep quiet.

"Just think, if that was your mother," Raina, one of the twins, says.

"I wouldn't even claim her if she *was* my moms," Char says, taking out deodorant. Then she pulls up her shirt and reaches inside to roll that sticky blue stuff on.

The four of us meet in the bathroom every morning. Me, Char, and the twins—Raina and Raise. We talk. Smoke. Stuff like that. I hang in the bathroom to get out of Momma's homemade rags and into the clothes Charlese brings for me to try on. Today, it's a skintight navy-blue jean dress, with thick gold buttons.

Char says the dress would look perfect if I had some hips and boobs to go with it. Char blows a fat ring of stinking gray smoke in my face. I laugh, like everybody else. You got to *go* along with Char if you want to *get* along with her. You can't be all sensitive. That's what Char says.

When the first period bell rings, I throw my backpack over my shoulders and head for class. Char and them are cutting class. Hanging out around the corner, probably. "I ain't for looking at that woman's mug today," Char says. "It's enough to make you throw up."

Char takes out another Kool cigarette, and taps it on her hand like she's giving herself a needle. She puts it in her mouth, and waits for Raise to light it. Then she closes her eyes, and sucks in the smoke slow and long like she's making a wish. The next thing I know, she's blowing smoke in my face again. I guess that's supposed to be funny. Char's laughing real hard. She tells me to get out her face. I do what I'm told.

I didn't always hang with Char. Last year, I hung by myself. I went to class. Got mostly A's. Nobody even noticed me till Caleb Jamaal Assam came along. Caleb's the smartest boy in school. Cute. Friendly. A poet. I should of known being with him was gonna cause me trouble.

He stared at me half the year. I thought he saw what everybody else saw. Skinny, poor, black Maleeka. But Caleb saw something different. He said I was pretty. Said he liked my eyes and sweet cocoa brown skin. He wrote me poems and letters. He put spearmint gum inside. Walked me to class. Gave me a ring. I ain't told Momma.

After a while, everybody knew. Charlese and them laughed when Caleb and I walked by. They'd stuck out their legs and tried to trip me. They wrote Caleb notes saying not even the Goodwill would want my clothes. Somebody said I had hair so nappy I needed a rake to comb it.

It was that class trip to Washington, D.C., where things really fell apart. Caleb sat next to me. They teased us all the way there. Barks came from the back of the bus. Spit bombs flew my way. Then John-John started singing his song. "Maleeka, Maleeka, we sure want to keep her but she so black, we just can't see her." The whole bus started in. Teachers tried to make them stop. By then, it was too late.

I looked at Caleb. He gave me the goofiest smile and said, "Sorry, Maleeka . . . ," and moved to the front of the bus with his boys. They slapped him five. Everybody laughed and clapped. I sat there with a frozen smile on my face like that stupid Mona Lisa. Till this day, I don't know nothing about Washington, D.C., just that I don't ever want to go there no more.

Things got worse after that. Kids picked on me more than ever. They sang John-John's stupid song whenever I walked the halls. They got on my case about every little thing. My hair. My clothes. My color. My good grades. The fact that teachers liked me.

I didn't want to go to school after a while, but Momma said I had to. So I came up with a plan. I went to Char and said if she would let me hang out with her, you know, kind of look out for me, I would do her homework and stuff. She laughed at first. Said for me to get out of her face. That she don't want no geeks hanging round her, especially no ugly ones. I didn't listen. I turned up everywhere she was. The bathroom. Lunchroom. The water fountain. I even did her homework a few times to show her I knew my stuff. She gave in after a while, and kids started leaving me alone. After that, Char started bringing clothes to school for me. "You got to look like something when you with me," she said, kicking a bag of stuff my way.

But even those hundred-dollar pants suits she brought in for me to wear can't make up for the hurt I feel when she slaps me with them mean words of hers.

CHAPTER FOUR

WHEN THE SECOND BELL RINGS, I run to Miss Saunders's class like somebody set my shoes on fire. It don't help none. Soon as I walk in, I know I'm in trouble. Everybody's got their head down and they're writing. Miss Saunders nods for me to take out paper and get to my seat. "What does your face say to the world?" is written on the blackboard. I laugh, only it comes out like a sneeze through my nose.

Miss Saunders is collecting papers before I even got three sentences down on my paper. She knows I just slipped in. That don't stop her from asking me to answer the question, though.

"My face?" I point to myself.

"Maleeka's face says she needs to stay out of the sun," Larry Baker says, covering his face with a book.

"Naw, man," Gregory Williams says. "Maleeka's face says, Black is beautiful."

Miss Saunders don't say nothing. She just crosses her arms and gets real quiet. She don't care if she done embarrassed me again.

"Maleeka?" she says.

I don't answer her question or look her way. I eye the ceiling and count the blobs of gum hanging there like pretty-colored snot.

"Can anybody else tell me what their face says to the world?" Miss Saunders asks. Her gold bangles jingle while she makes her way around the room. Miss Saunders is as quiet as a tiger sneaking up on its supper. It's them Italian leather shoes of hers, I guess.

Malcolm Moore raises his hand. Malcolm is fine. He's got long, straight hair. Skin the color of a butterscotch milkshake. Gray, sad eyes. He's half and half—got a white dad and a black momma. He's lucky. He looks more like his dad than his mom.

"My face says I'm all that," Malcolm says, rubbing them six chin hairs he calls a beard. "It says to the homies, I'm the doctor of love. I'm good *to* ya and good *for* ya."

Everybody laughs. Faith, his girlfriend of the week, throws a pencil across the room. It bounces off the back of his chair, and lands between his big feet. Miss

Saunders gives Faith the eye, letting her know to cut it out.

When the laughing's done, hands go up. Some folks say funny stuff about their face. Others is real serious. Like John-John. He says his face tells the world he doesn't take no stuff. That people better respect him, or else. I never seen nothing like that in John-John's face. He looks more scared than mean. I guess there ain't no accounting for what folks see in their own mirrors.

When Miss Saunders asks, "What's my face say?" don't nobody say nothing.

"Don't get all closed-mouthed, now," she says. "I hear you whispering in the hall. Laughing at me." She walks the aisles again. She stops by me and sits on my desk. "Faces say more than you think. Even mine. Don't be shy. Say what's on your mind."

My hand goes up. I figure she's embarrassed me twice since she's been here this week. Now it's her turn. "Not to hurt your feelings . . . but . . . I think it says, you know, you're a freak."

"That's cold," Chrystal Johnson says, frowning.

Miss Saunders put her hands up to her chin like she's praying. She gets up and walks the room, pacing. We don't say nothing. We just listen to the clock tick. Shuffle our papers. Watch for some reaction from Miss Saunders.

"Freak," she says. "I saw that too when I was young."

Then she explains how she was born with her face like that. How when she was little her parents had the preacher pray over it, the old folks work their roots on it, and her grandmother use some concoction to change the color of that blotch on her cheek so it matched the rest of her skin. Miss Saunders says none of the stuff she tried on her face worked. So she finally figured she'd better love what God gave her.

"Liking myself didn't come overnight," she says. "I took a lot of wrong turns to find out who I really was. You will, too." Everybody starts talking at once, asking her questions. Miss Saunders answers 'em all. Some kids even go up to her face and stare and point. She lets them do it too, like she's proud of her face or something.

Then Miss Saunders comes over to my desk and stares down at me. "It takes a long time to accept yourself for who you are. To see the poetry in your walk," she says, shaking her hips like she's doing some African dance. Kids bust out laughing. "To look in the mirror and like what you see, even when it doesn't look like anybody else's idea of beauty."

For a minute, it seems like Miss Saunders is getting all spacey on us. Like her mind is somewhere else. Then she's back, talking that talk. "So, what's my face say to the world?" she asks. "My face says I'm smart. Sassy. Sexy.

Self-confident," she says, snapping her fingers rapid-fire. "It says I'm caring and, yes, even a little cold sometimes. See these laugh lines," she says, almost poking herself in the eyes. "They let people know that I love a good joke. These tiny bags? They tell the world I like to stay up late."

"Doing *what*, Miss Saunders?" John-John asks. "Checking homework, or making out?"

Miss Saunders throws her head back and laughs. The lines around her eyes crinkle. The bangles on her arm jingle. "What do I think my face says to the world? I think it says I'm *all that*," she says, snapping her fingers.

Kids clap like they just seen a good movie, and they yell stuff like: "Go on, Miss Saunders."

"Give me five."

"Tell us who you really is."

Miss Saunders quiets everybody down, then starts telling us more about herself. She's a big shot at an advertising agency downtown. A few months ago, her company and the school board came up with a new program that lets professionals take a leave of absence for a year to teach in inner-city schools. She says she always wanted to teach. She says being at McClenton Middle School will help her figure out if she wants to make a career out of teaching.

The next thing we know, Miss Saunders is asking us to take out some paper for a test. A surprise test. Some of the kids who was just giving out high fives are singing a different tune now. Worm thinks Miss Saunders is playing around for a minute. But she ain't. She says she wants to evaluate us. You know, to figure out what we know and don't know.

Miss Saunders says the test won't count for a grade. John-John starts to get smart, he don't do so good on tests. "Then why we got to do it?" he asks, putting one leg across his desk.

Miss Saunders struts over to his desk, and pushes his leg off. "Because I say so," she says, handing out the papers and telling us to settle down.

CHAPTER FIVE

WHEN I GET HOME, MOMMA is waiting at the door to take me downtown to buy new clothes. She says she got a bonus at work, so she has some extra cash to throw around for once. I don't care how she got the money, just as long as I get to spend some of it. So here I am today, looking fine. I got on enough lip gloss to shine a car and I have a crease in my pants sharp enough to cut somebody. For the first time in who knows when, I look like somebody, and Charlese Jones ain't had nothing to do with it.

At school, everybody's staring at me. Even John-John's doing a double-take. When I walk into class, all eyes is on me. Char's the only one that's got something negative to say.

"So your momma finally broke down and bought you some clothes. About time," she says, as soon as we get to Miss Saunders's class.

When I walk in Miss Saunders's room, she's already giving out an assignment. We get to work on this assignment with someone else, she says. Char lets Miss Saunders know that me and her are gonna be partners. Char's figuring I'll do all the work. But Miss Saunders is hip to that game. She says *she's* picking our partners. She hooks me up with Desda. Char don't like that one bit. She picks up her stuff and walks out the room. Miss Saunders acts like Char's leaving don't bother her none.

Desda is the short, fat girl sitting by the door. Everybody in school knows she can cook up a storm. Turkey, stuffed chicken, gravy, three-cheese macaroni, pasta salad, fried steak, lasagna. She's won all kinds of cooking awards. She even won five hundred dollars from a Pillsbury Bake-Off contest. She called her receipe Desda Darling's Delicious Double-Dutch Chocolate Chip Cake.

She never will spend the five-hundred-dollar prize money, though. It's scholarship money for college, and Desda can't hardly read what the award says, let alone try to get into college. I hear Miss Saunders's gonna start tutoring Desda. Yeah, right, I'm thinking Desda's gonna read on grade level when pigs fly.

Anyhow, Miss Saunders asks the class to pretend we're teenagers living in the seventeenth century. We have to write a diary "chronicling" our experiences. John-John raises his hand and asks why we got to do this assignment anyway. "Don't make no sense to me," he says, frowning.

Miss Saunders looks like she's thinking hard for a good reason herself. Her fingers go up on her lips. Her eyes check out the ceiling like she's gonna find the answer up there. "I want you to know what it feels like to live in somebody else's skin and to see the world through somebody else's eyes," she says.

Miss Saunders takes a deep breath. Closes her eyes. Then tells us to do the same. "When you were little, you loved to play pretend. To be G.I. Joe or Barbie. This is the same thing. Playing pretend," she says.

"G.I. Joe's a punk. Don't nobody wanna be him," John-John yells, cracking up the whole class.

"You get to be anyone you like," Miss Saunders says, walking toward him. She tells us that this is an exercise that will show her how well we write and use our imaginations. So no more grumbling, she says. "Get to work. Now."

I look at Desda. She's sitting there showing off her big white teeth, and licking her lips like they're candy.

At first, I don't say nothing. I roll my pencil around on the desk. I wait for Desda to start things. But nothing happens. Desda doesn't say nothing for ten whole minutes. Then here comes Miss Saunders like she's Big Ben, the clock. "I hope you and your partner are using your time wisely. You only have twenty minutes left."

I rip out some loose-leaf paper and start writing. "This here's what we're going to do," I tell Desda. She doesn't say nothing. She is just smiling and picking at some crud caked in her eyes. So I get started without her.

At first, I pretend I'm a girl living in a drafty castle that I hate because my parents don't got enough candles to light the place. Then I start thinking. Back then, I would of been a slave. Maybe a slave girl in the bottom of a boat, chained to some boy with the prettiest eyes and some girl who keeps stealing my little scraps of food. Skinny and stinking and starving and all the time next to a cute boy who I like so much, it hurts. I start to write:

Dear Diary:

I hate fish, but I could eat a whale right now. I haven't had nothing much to eat for three weeks . . . or is it five weeks? Watery rice with maggots in it is all they give us here. Momma used to always say I was the skinny one. She would cry if she saw me now. All ribs and knees. Ankles, big as yams.

Worse than no food and stink everywhere is having Kinjari see me now. Momma would say I am a vain and foolish girl. Here dying and wondering what some boy thinks about me. But I can't help it. In my village,

25

Kinjari's family would know my family and maybe arrange for us to be married. Even at my age—thirteen. But no one would ask to marry me like this. Sitting in my own filth. My head shaved clean to keep lice away. Skin dry and ashy like tree bark ate away by the desert wind.

Day in and day out Kinjari eyes me, staring like he sees the sun rising in my eyes. I want to ask him why he looks at me that way. Am I something so beautiful he can't help but stare? I keep quiet. Beauty is where one finds it, my father used to say. Sometimes, when I wake, I am so close to Kinjari I can smell his breath. Like mine, it is awful. But I don't care. It is good knowing he is near. Knowing he was near, I mean.

I was sick, bad, for a long while. When I woke up, Kinjari was gone. Dead. "He had the mark. The pocks," the girl chained to me said, sucking her front teeth like they was soup bones. "The slavers tossed him over the side," she said.

But this one, she steals my food. Can I trust her with the truth? I don't know.

—Akeelma

I read the diary letter to Desda. She asks how I came up with the girl's name, Akeelma? It's close to my name spelled backward, I tell her.

"How come you don't talk proper, like Akeelma talks in her diary?" she asks.

"Don't nobody talk like that for real, only people in old movies and books." Then I tell her how, before he died, my father read me books where people spoke like that. "Some of it stuck, I guess."

Miss Saunders picks up the papers and starts reading some out loud.

Don't read mine, I think, turning my head to the wall.

Desda raises her hand and asks Miss Saunders to read ours. Miss Saunders says it's the best, most thoughtful piece she's heard so far. "Desda, Maleeka, good job," she says.

Desda smiles. She sits up straight and tall and shows off them giant teeth of hers. I should be pissed off at her, since she didn't do a dang thing to help me write my essay. But today I've got on my new clothes and I'm feeling mighty fine. I don't crack on Desda, or nothing. I just get myself on out of there. I don't even answer Char when she calls for me to come her way. This is my day, and I'm not letting nobody spoil it. Nobody.

Miss Saunders has got other ideas, though. She pulls me and Desda aside and says she wants us to keep doing the assignment. No one else, just us. Desda asks what we gonna get out of it. Extra credit is all. *Hummph*. Desda pulls out right then. Admits she didn't have nothing much to do with writing the assignment. That I did all the work. Miss Saunders turns around to me. Desda walks off.

I don't know. Maybe it's these new clothes and all. But I say OK. I don't want to spoil my good mood by telling no teacher where to get off today. Besides, I liked writing that stuff. I didn't tell that to Miss Saunders, though. She could use it against me, somehow.

CHAPTER SIX

ONE MINUTE I'M WALKING DOWN THE hall watching people watching me in my new clothes. The next minute Daphne Robinson is all up in my face ready to fight. She's saying she just found out I was kissing her boyfriend in the hall the other day. "Worm wasn't sucking my lips off. He was kissing Charlese," I want to yell. But I don't. Bad things happen around here to people who can't keep their mouth shut.

I keep stepping, and tell Daphne she's got the wrong girl. But I ain't as cool as I seem. My fingers are starting to shake, and my throat is dry as toast. Daphne's itching for a fight. I can feel it. The next thing I know, she's grabbing hold of my braids. She got them wrapped around her hands like boxing tape and is punching me upside the head with them.

I am taller than Daphne, so it seems like all I have to do is reach down and slap her off me like a bug. I'm pushing her away as best I can. Only every time I do it, it feels like my hair is being ripped from my scalp.

Kids are yelling all around me. "Beat her butt good. Ain't nobody got the right to steal your man." Teachers say to break it up and for kids to move so they can stop this thing.

Char's just standing there eating a candy bar like she's at the movies. I'm eyeing her, hoping maybe she'll jump in or at least say she was the one that was kissing Worm. She digs the chocolate out from between her teeth and takes another bite of candy.

All of a sudden here comes Miss Saunders, pushing her way past everybody to where me and Daphne are fighting. I never thought I'd be so glad to see that woman. But I am. She's pushing her way through the crowd, like there ain't nobody at McClenton big or bad enough to stop her. I don't know what's got into me, I ain't no fighter. Never fought one day in my life. But all of a sudden, I'm feeling strong when I see Miss Saunders headed my way. So I raise my hand in the air and give Daphne some of what she been giving me. Next thing I know, Miss Saunders's grabbing hold of my hand, telling me to cut it out. Big mistake. Now Daphne's got the chance to get in one last hit. She takes her hand, the one with Worm's dad's big basketball ring on it, and smacks me across my face. My cheek puffs up like hot cookie dough. I can feel the blood oozing down to my chin.

Miss Saunders shoves her hands in her suit pocket and pulls out tissues like she's got boxes of them stashed away. The principal starts breaking up the crowd, telling everyone to move along or come to his office. Next thing I know, Daphne's gathering up snot in her throat like she's summoning up demons. Before I even think about it, that big, green slimy stuff comes flying my way, landing right on my shirt. Charlese is one of the first people to crack up.

The principal, Mr. Pajolli, has got Daphne by the arm and is telling her to come to his office. Miss Saunders has got them tissues, rubbing blood and snot off me, still holding my arm like I'm gonna do something dangerous.

"Get off me," I say, jerking my arm away. "Why don't you go back to where you come from?"

"That will be enough," Mr. Pajolli says, heading my way.

"What's she doing here anyway, Mr. P.?" I say, holding my face. "She don't know what she's doing."

Mr. Pajolli takes me by the elbow and tells some kid to get me to the nurse's office. He takes Daphne with him. She's mouthing off, saying if she gets suspended, I better, too.

Miss Saunders has got her arms raised, telling people to get to class. Me, I'm just wondering when she's gonna get out my life.

CHAPTER SEVEN

NO TELEVISION, TELEPHONE, OR HANGING OUT with friends
for three weeks, all because of that fight. And that ain't
even the worse part. The principal, Miss Saunders, and
Momma got their heads together and came up with a way
to punish me good. They say it ain't punishment, but it
sure feels that way. They found me a job. A job that don't
pay no money and ain't no fun at all. I don't even want
it. But Momma's got her mind set, so that's that.

I will be working in the school office, filing papers,
stapling letters, that kind of stuff. This is Miss Saunders's
bright idea. She talked it over with Momma last night
on the telephone. I could hear some of the conversation
coming through the receiver. Miss Saunders was saying something about me wasting my potential. That the
school needed a better way to keep up with me so I don't

fall through the cracks. And Momma believes all that crap, when the truth is that Miss Saunders is just a big mouth, bossy broad who likes to throw her weight around and treat everybody like they are some broken pot she's got to patch up.

I could smell the peppermint tea Momma was sipping, while she spoke to Miss Saunders. "Maleeka's got more potential than she's letting on. Keeping her under the principal's nose may be just the way to get her back in line."

Momma and Miss Saunders talk a long time. When they're done, I try to tell Momma that Miss Saunders doesn't know what she's doing. That she ain't even a real teacher. Momma says she doesn't care. She likes her.

"That Miss Saunders is the first teacher who ever called here to talk about what was going on with you. I like that. It shows she's concerned, that this job ain't just about the money."

I tell Momma that Miss Saunders don't need the money. She got plenty. "Don't it make you wonder, Momma, why somebody with all that money and a good job would give it up to come to McClenton?"

Momma sits there for a while, thinking. "I wouldn't think on it too much, Maleeka," she says. "She's here, that's the important thing."

No way is Momma gonna let me not work in that office. She even threatens me, saying if I try to get out of it she will take away all my rights at home. So I figured, cool. I'll do it. And while I'm doing it, I will find out the real deal on Miss Saunders. Get all up in her business like she's up in mine. Payback, you know.

So on the first day I work in the office, I ask Miss Carol, the secretary, about Miss Saunders. Miss Carol likes to gossip, so I figure she'll tell me something.

But Miss Carol just stares up at me with her arms crossed. "You're here to work, right?"

"Right," I say, biting on the dry skin hanging from my lip.

"Then do your work and stop minding grown folks' business."

Maxine, the other girl working in the office, is acting like she's filing papers. I know she's listening, though. I leave Miss Carol standing there with her arms folded, and I file my stuff like she says. Turns out, I don't need her to tell me about Miss Saunders. It don't take me long to start piecing stuff together from the other teachers. They complain about her every chance they get.

"If you ask me, that program doesn't work one bit," Mr. Mac, the science teacher, says. "A school doesn't run like a corporation. Things don't happen at the snap of a finger or the drop of a pen. Change takes time."

"A bull in a china shop, that's what she is," Miss Benson, the librarian, says under her breath. "She's not following the curriculum the way it's laid out. She's pushing the kids too hard. Telling them to read fifty pages one night, thirty pages the next. I'm telling you, hiring her was a bad move."

If those teachers knew I was working at the desk, they would be more careful. But they don't know I'm here. I've dropped some paper clips on the floor and I'm crouching under a desk to pick them up slowly. It looks like nobody's around but Miss Carol, and she's in the back Xeroxing. Maxine is running errands. When I stand up, Mr. Mac gets all red-faced. He thinks I'm trying to be a smart aleck. His lips curl up tight. "My, my, Maleeka, aren't you the lucky one? Here to work in the office, I see," he says, stomping out the door, right into Mr. Pajolli, who's heard everything he's said.

"Sometimes, Mr. Mac, you need new ideas, to do things differently. Nothing wrong with a little change, is there?" he asks.

"I'm sorry, Mr. Pajolli, but the way I see it, rewarding those who misbehave and refuse to play by the rules is wrong. Dead wrong. How will you reward the good ones, put them on detention?" Mr. Mac asks.

"They're all good ones, Mr. Mac. Some of them just need more support than others."

Mr. Mac makes a clicking noise with his tongue. He and Miss Benson walk down the hall together side by side. We all think those two got a thing going on, even though we never seen them kiss or even hold hands.

Mr. Pajolli tells me not to worry. That things will work out fine for me if I try hard enough. All the time he's talking, I'm trying to figure out how I can cut this gig loose. I mean, let's face it, I got better things to do with my time than work for free.

CHAPTER EIGHT

THE ONLY REASON MOMMA LETS ME off restriction at home is because I started that new job, and she thinks that's gonna change me somehow. I don't tell her she's out of her head. Shoot, I'm just glad I can watch TV and talk on the phone again. After all, it *is* Saturday.

But I can't talk on the phone right this minute because as soon as my girl Sweets comes over to my house, she hogs the phone. Sweets's momma is super-strict. She *never* lets Sweets on the phone. So here she is, laying across my bed on her stomach, with her short legs waving in the air every time Larry says something to her.

Neither one of us is supposed to talk to boys. But we do every once in a while. With the way Sweets is acting, you'd think Larry could see her. She's putting lip gloss on her lips, combing her hair, brushing off her clothes.

Sweets has been liking Larry since she was six years old. She thinks he likes her, only he's so shy, you can't tell. All he ever talks about with her is basketball. They're talking about the game the Knicks won the other night. If you could see that big smile Sweets has got on her face, you would think Larry's just said he loves her.

Sweets and me been best friends since kindergarten. She goes to the school across town, the school for smart girls with attitudes, she likes to say. I could have gone there. My grades were as good as Sweets's. Better, in fact. Only I changed my mind at the last minute. I went to the interview and wouldn't answer one question they asked. Momma was so embarrassed. She cried all the way on the subway ride home.

I didn't plan it that way. I just froze, I guess. The school is so big. So clean. So fancy. And them girls . . . they looked like they come out of a magazine. Long, straight hair. Skin the color of potato chips and cashews and Mary Jane candies. No Almond Joy–colored girls like me. No gum-smacking, wisecracking girls from my side of town.

That didn't bother Sweets none. She says she deserves to be in that school as much as anyone.

"You got the right color skin," I said, poking her fat tan face.

"It's not about color," she said. "It's how you feel about

who you are that counts. Hummph," she said, twirling around on her toes like a ballerina with bad feet. "I'm as good as the queen of England, the president of the United States, and ten movie stars, all rolled into one. So they better let me in that there school or else," she said, shaking her fist up to the sky. I guess Sweets's attitude paid off. They let her into that high-toned school.

Up till last year, Sweets and me did everything together. Now all she does is study. "I gotta keep up," she says. "Getting straight A's in this school, ain't like getting A's in our old school. You sweat to get these A's. Gotta half die to keep 'em."

Sweets been on the phone for a half hour already. I tell her to cut it. She says to give her five more minutes. That really means fifteen minutes, so I go back to doing what I am doing. Looking at all the junk I got under my bed. Socks. Cards. Dust. An earring I've been looking for. A piece of old, hard toast. And a mirror I ain't seen for a while. It's a cheap little thing. But Daddy gave it to me a long time ago, so I try to hold onto it. It's got a pink plastic handle with little white bunnies painted on it.

I check my face out in the mirror. That cut from Daphne's ring is gone. Momma says I'm like Daddy. I heal fast. That ain't the only thing Daddy and me got in common. I got his eyes. Dark, almond-shaped eyes with long, thick black lashes.

My lips, they're like Momma's. Full and wide. They look like that actor's lips on TV. I can't think of his name, just now. But he's got the kind of lips that make you want to kiss him quick. Soft, smooth, pretty-looking lips. My nose and my ears, I don't know where they came from. They don't look like Momma's *or* Daddy's. My nose is small and pug. Daddy used to always pinch it when I was little.

I am the same color Daddy was. When I was little, he would come home from work and say, "I sure could use me a warm cup of cocoa." That meant for me to give him a big hug and lots of kisses. I liked that.

I didn't used to mind being this color. Then kids started teasing me about it. Making me feel like something was wrong with how I look. And when Daddy passed away, that just made things worse.

I stare at myself for maybe twenty minutes in Daddy's mirror. I don't get it. I think I'm kind of nice-looking. Why don't other people see what I see? I think. Out of the blue I get an idea. I'm gonna cut my hair. Cut it real short like the girl on the cover of the magazine laying on my floor. I yell for Sweets to get off the phone. She ain't listening. She's smiling at something Larry just said to her.

"Off the phone," I yell so he can hear. "Off the phone, before I tell Larry you like—"

Before I finish the sentence Sweets is hanging up and hitting me over the head with a pillow. "You know that ain't right," she says, whacking me good.

I tell Sweets I'm gonna cut my hair. Gonna cut it real close. "People gonna see I ain't who I used to be," I say.

"You gonna cut your hair off, like bald?" Sweets asks.

"Well, not that off. But close, like this," I say, showing her the picture.

Sweets helps me take out my braids, and lets me know that I shouldn't be trying nothing like this by myself. "If you jack up your hair, you really will look a mess," she says.

Then she tells me how her cousin Ronnie just opened up a shop on the avenue. "I don't have money to go to no shop," I tell her. Sweets says that her cousin did her hair for free last week, and all she had to do was sweep up the floor.

Sweets calls her cousin for me, and her cousin says yeah. She will cut my hair, but I have to give her three Saturdays' worth of work. And I have to bring a note from Momma saying the cut is OK with her. It takes me two hours to talk Momma into this thing. I don't tell Sweets or Momma the real reason that I'm doing this. That I want a new look like that model in the magazine, so that maybe people will start to see me differently and treat me differently. Momma and Sweets wouldn't understand me saying nothing like that. So I just keep my mouth shut, while Sweets and I walk to the avenue. Ronnie tells me to leave things to her. She puts a texturizer on my scalp, till it loosens up my hair, then she washes the texturizer out. When she is finished, it seems like ten thousand tiny black shiny curls was all over my head.

Ronnie takes out the clippers, gives me some points on the side, and evens up the back of my hairline.

"Hmmm," she says. "Now, you got to have a little attitude when you wear this cut. You got attitude, Maleeka?" she asks, with her hands on her hips.

I look at her and ask what she means.

Then a woman comes out from under the dryer. She takes off her clip-on earrings and asks Ronnie for some alcohol. She cleans them clunky things off and clips them on my ears without even asking me.

"This is one of those hairdos you strut your stuff in. Sisters wearing these know they're sharp," Ronnie says, taking out the clippers and going at my hairline again.

I'm looking in the mirror, and I can't believe my eyes. I *like* what I see.

"You got any lip gloss?" she asks me, turning me around in the chair, still checking out my hair.

I dig in my pocketbook and pull out some red lipstick from Murphy's Drugstore.

"You're too young to be wearing lipstick," Ronnie says. She makes me stick my finger in the gigantic jar of Vaseline she keeps near her mirror, and I rub a little on my lips. When Ronnie's finished, the three other hairdressers get all up in my face, and so do some customers. One woman's got relaxer cream all over her head. They're all talking about how good I look. Sweets is nodding and smiling and agreeing with everybody.

"Give me some attitude," Ronnie says, taking off my cape.

I have my head down and my arms crossed. Another woman comes out from under the dryer and starts strutting across the floor.

"Attitude, girl," she says, switching her butt around, dipping and turning like a fashion model.

"Attitude," Sweets says, getting into the act.

Everybody turns and looks at me. I start snapping my fingers and walking around like I'm somebody. I look *good*. The woman who's given me her earrings comes over to me and puts her hands on my hips. "You got to shake 'em hard. Make people know you mean business."

I start pushing my hips from side to side, taking long steps and putting my arms out like I'm on a runway some-place.

"You go, girl," a woman says. "Shake it. Shake it, don't break it."

"You do look good, Maleeka," Sweets agrees. "That cut is you."

A new customer comes into the store and over to Ronnie. The woman with the earrings gets herself back under the dryer, and the other lady goes back to getting her relaxer washed out. I get Ronnie's broom and start sweeping up.

CHAPTER NINE

ON MONDAY MS. ALLEN, THE art teacher, does a double take when I walk into her class. I know she wants to ask me what happened, but teachers can't always just come out and ask you stuff like that. Kids, they're different. As soon as I walked into the school building they were all over me, wanting to know why I didn't have no hair.

I expect John-John not to like the cut. I mean, what does he like about me, anyhow? Nothing. And I expect Charlese and the twins to say they don't like it, even if they secretly do.

In third period, kids really light into me. By fourth period, I'm wearing the baseball cap I brought from home, just in case. Mr. Klein, the social studies teacher, tells me to take off the hat, but I give him some lame excuse and he lets me keep it on. The next thing I know, somebody's yanking off the hat and making cracks about my peanut head.

I don't get it. I mean, I look good. I *know* I do. Desda comes up to me and says I shouldn't let them get to me. I tell her I'll check her later. I go to the bathroom. Nobody's in there yet. I look in the mirror and start crying. "You know, Maleeka," I hear myself say, "you can glue on some hair, paint yourself white, come to school wearing a leather coat down to your toes and somebody will still say something mean to hurt your feelings. That's how it goes at this school."

I walk around that bathroom trying to think of what to do. I start reading some of the stuff on the walls.

"Char and Worm 4-ever."

"Wash me."

"If you like school, you stupid."

I sit myself up on one of the sinks, and think back to Saturday when I got my hair cut.

Tears come to my eyes when I put my hands on my head and feel my little bit of hair. I mean, I know I asked for it, and that it looked good at Ronnie's place, but seeing it in the school bathroom mirror is something else.

I jump off the sink and lean close to the mirror on the wall, and think of Daddy. "Maleeka," he used to say, "you got to see yourself with your own eyes. That's the only way you gonna know who you really are."

I reach down into my bag and pull out the little hand mirror Daddy gave me and look at myself real good. My nose is running. I blow it and throw the tissue away. I splash some water on my face and pat it dry. I reach deep down into my pocketbook and pull out the little jar of Vaseline and shine up my lips. Then I ball up my cap, stuff it in my backpack, and walk right on out of there.

CHAPTER TEN

WE NEED A NEW ALARM CLOCK. Ours rings whenever it wants. Two in the morning. Ten at night. It don't matter. But you can be sure of one thing, it ain't never gonna ring when it's supposed to.

When Momma comes in my room telling me I'm gonna be late if I don't get a move on, I ain't surprised. It's the third time this week I'm late because of that clock. So I just ignore Momma, pull my quilt up over my head, and turn over.

Momma does what she always does. She pulls the covers off and threatens to yank down the sheet.

"I'm up. I'm up." I sit on the edge of the bed. Hands folded. Head drooping. My eyes are still closed when Momma goes back downstairs to cook breakfast. I wash up, then look through my closet for some jeans or something.

I push my way past that new shirt Momma made, and hope she don't ask me about it. I don't want to hurt her feelings, but one shoulder is higher than the other one. She fixed it three times already, but it just ain't working. I don't want to tell her that, though.

Sweets asks me all the time why I don't just tell Momma I don't want to wear her stuff. But I can't. Momma needs to keep sewing. If she don't, I ain't sure what's gonna happen to her.

When I finally get to the kitchen table, the oatmeal's cold and slick, like Silly Putty. I eat dry toast instead. Momma gives me the once-over. She comes and straightens up my turtleneck collar. She made this one too, but the woman across the street helped her with it, so it ain't so bad.

Momma is dressed in a blue uniform. Today she got herself some different kind of tea. It smells more like chicken noodle soup to me. She's stirring it and stirring it, but not drinking it. I kiss her quick on the side of the head. She don't even notice. She's eyeing the newspaper like she does every morning. Two newspapers are spread wide open on the kitchen table. Every once in a while, pages slide onto the floor, or get greasy from some eggs or bacon Momma eats while she's reading.

Momma's always got to know what's happening in the

stock market. She sews my clothes to save money so that she can play the stocks. She thinks we'll be rich one day, but she never invests any money. By the time she gets a few hundred dollars saved up here and there, the pipes start leaking or the roof needs fixing. Or Momma gets one of her dreams, where some dead relative comes back and tells her to play the lottery and put all her money on some number they told her about, like 557, 810, or 119. It never fails. Momma loses all the money. Every dime. But that's the kind of luck we have—dumb dead relatives who go outta their way to interrupt your good-night's sleep to give you a lucky number that only brings you bad luck. Now who needs that?

Momma never gives up, though. She's always looking for new ways to make money. She's sold Tupperware, magazines, and pretty junk for kitchen walls. We're still poor as dirt.

A lot of folks think Momma don't have all her marbles. I can tell by the way they talk to her, kind of loud—like folks do with crazy people—with a smirk on their face, like they know a secret she don't. But the joke's on them. Momma's the smartest person in the world. She's a math whiz and can add numbers faster than anybody I know.

Sometime she embarrasses me. She's the type of woman that will put down her groceries and jump rope with eight-year-old kids on the street. She will play stick ball with the boys in the neighborhood and argue with the winos on the corner over who's gonna win the next election. Sometimes, my friends laugh at Momma. But when I start to complain, Sweets and them tell me to shut up. They know, like I do, ain't no one in the neighborhood gotta heart bigger than my Momma.

I blow a kiss to Momma and I rush past her and head for school. She says in the only French she knows, "*Je t'aime ma petite.* I love you my little one," and then she goes back to her stocks. I hear her mumbling something about General Electric stock falling twenty points. I have no idea what that means. Ain't sure Momma does neither.

CHAPTER ELEVEN

McCLENTON MIDDLE SCHOOL AIN'T THE KIND of place where you want the lunch ladies mad at you. No matter how bad the food looks, or smells, you best keep your mouth shut. If you don't, you can end up with hair in your spaghetti. Pencil shavings in your pizza. Pepper in your milk.

But something's got into Charlese today. She acts like them lunch ladies won't cause her no trouble. When she goes through the line, she says the hamburgers look like burnt dog doo-doo. Miss Brown, the lunch lady who's serving, don't say nothing. She just clears her throat and runs her hands through her short gray hair. By the time Charlese gets out the line, there it is. Lettuce in her milk. Dried-up food on her fork. Something indescribable on her hamburger bun. Me and her can't figure out what it is, but we think it used to be alive.

I bring my own lunch from home, and I tell Char she can have it. Today I got a bologna sandwich. Char don't want no part of it. She slams her lunch tray down on the table. The whole place gets quiet. "They better give me some decent food," she yells loud enough for all the lunch ladies to hear. Miss Brown just keeps stirring peas and wiping sweat.

"Move out of my way," Char says to a girl sitting at the table. She don't even give the girl a chance to move before she flicks a handful of them greasy, rock-hard peas in her face, then dares her to say something about it.

The girl knows what's good for her. She wipes the slimy pea juice off her chin and moves on.

"Serves you right," Char says, drying her wet hands on my backpack. "Next time, she'll get out of my way before I ask."

"They gonna give me what I paid for," Char says. She shoves her lunch tray at me so fast, it almost slides off the table. "Take it back, Maleeka. Tell 'em I want another plate—now."

I look at Charlese like she's crazy. "They won't take it from me. You know that, Char," I say, in a dry, shaky voice.

Charlese doesn't say nothing at first. She just stares at me without blinking for the longest time. "Do I have to jack you up right here in front of everybody?" she asks, slapping one of the twins five.

"I said you could have my bologna sandwich," I say. But Char turns to me with her hands on her hips and a face that says, "I know you ain't talking to me."

I don't have no choice. I pick up her tray and get back in line. It seems like twenty kids are in front of me. By the time I get to Miss Brown again, my stomach is growling.

Miss Brown ain't smiling one little bit when she sees Char's tray. I tell her what the problem is. She says she'll take back the food, only not from me. Char starts yelling at me from way back in the lunchroom. Everybody can hear her. A teacher tells her to shut up, but the teacher can't make Char's eyes stop digging into me.

Miss Brown cuts me a break, and starts throwing the old food in the trash. I stop her when she gets to the hamburger bun with that stuff on top. "Leave it," I say quietly. She looks like she wants to say something else, then she waves her hand at me, looks at the kid in the line after me, and says, "Next."

Char's yelling, "Hurry up, Maleeka." I take the tray with the same old hamburger bun on it over to the side of the cafeteria where the ketchup and mustard packs are. I scrape the yuck off the top of the bun, and smear it on top of Char's hamburger. Then I squeeze ketchup and mustard on the meat, and take the whole thing to Char.

Char snatches the tray out of my hand. She opens up

the hamburger bun, and picks up the meat. She puts it to her nose and sniffs it like she does to all of her food. Then she drops the burger back on the bun and covers it with the other piece of bread.

"What? You think she spit in it?" Raina asks. "*Please.* Just eat so we can go."

Char laughs and takes a big bite. "Get lost, Maleeka," she says, with her mouth full. I don't ask no questions. I pick up my lunch bag and head for another table with this big grin on my face.

Desda is over in the corner by herself, so I go and sit with her. Soon as I get there, my sandwich falls out of the paper bag and onto the floor. Momma loves salad oil. She thinks it's good for your heart. Sometimes, like today, she gets a little heavy-handed with it. And it leaks all over the place.

Desda leans down and picks up my sandwich and hands it to me. I wipe off the cellophane with a tissue, unwrap it, and start eating.

While my mouth is stuffed with bologna and bread, Caleb comes over and starts telling me how good I look. Oil is oozing out the sides of my mouth as quick as I can wipe it off. Caleb don't seem to notice, he just keeps right on talking.

"I need to talk to you, Maleeka," he says, taking a napkin and wiping some oil off my chin.

I tell Caleb I've got to talk to him some other time. That me and Desda are going over homework right now. He says he'll talk to me later, and heads out of the lunchroom. Charlese stops him before he goes. She's all up in his face. He doesn't pay her no mind, he just keeps on stepping. Sometimes I can't help but wonder if Charlese wants Caleb because she knows he wants me.

Desda acts like I really meant what I said about her and me doing homework. She starts asking me if I've done the math homework—which I haven't, of course. But that don't stop Desda. She pulls out the homework anyhow and asks me ten thousand questions about the math problems. They are easy as pie, and I tell her so. Before I know it, I'm doing the work for her.

"If the homework's so easy, why didn't you do it last night?" she wants to know.

"Don't go there," I say.

"I worked on them problems for three hours straight," Desda says, stuffing chips in her mouth. "After that, I finally gave up and started watching TV." Desda's homework paper starts to spot from her greasy fingers.

Twenty minutes later we head for the door. Char's still sitting at the front of the cafeteria. Boys are crowded around, so that all you can see is them purple shoes of hers and that tight, black designer skirt. When she stands up to leave, one boy puts his arms round her waist and whispers something in her ear. She laughs, but you can tell she's faking it. She puts on her sunglasses, and walks toward the door with them boys following her like she's a movie star.

Before she leaves, she looks over my way and pulls her sunglasses down past her nose, so they're leaning on her top lip. She stares me down, then whispers something to one of the twins, and keeps on stepping.

"Ignore her," Desda says. The next thing I know, Raise is coming my way.

"Char wants to know if you've done her math?"

I reach in my book bag and pull out some papers. Char and them are in a different math class than me. It's a class for kids who don't have a clue what's going on. I hand the homework to Raise. "I didn't have time to do the social studies," I say, lying through my teeth. The social studies paper is still in my bag. It's the first time I don't give Char what she's asked for.

"Did you do mine and my sister's?" Raise wants to know.

I hand the other math papers to her.

As we leave the lunchroom, Desda says I shouldn't do nothing for them. "Yeah, right," I say.

CHAPTER TWELVE

THE NEXT DAY I'M WAITING IN the bathroom seems like forever. No Char. She's punishing me for getting out my place yesterday, I guess. When Char says come, you come. When she says do this for me, you do it, or else bad stuff happens. I didn't give Char her social studies homework yesterday, so no clothes for me today. Now I got to go to class in Momma's things or wear the clothes Char gave me yesterday. I got them here in my backpack. They're folded small as a bag of bread. They're wrinkled worse than Caleb's grandmomma's face, though.

I don't have much choice, so I keep on my own clothes. I stretch my arms toward the mirror. Not bad. Sleeves is even. Buttons sewed on straight. The seam down the shirt sleeve is crooked, is all. Could be worse.

I'm thinking maybe I'll skip class. Miss Saunders gave

me this here book the other day. *Life of a Slave Girl*, it's called. She said maybe it would help me with my writing. I've already read it twice. I stayed up all night reading it two days ago. I read it with a flashlight under the covers so Momma wouldn't holler. That book made me cry. It made me think about Akeelma and what was waiting for her once the boat docked.

While I'm still deciding if I'm gonna skip class, I tell myself that I'm only going to read *Life of a Slave Girl* for five minutes. The next thing I know, the late bell is ringing. I'm shoving that book in my book bag and running down the hall.

"Walk, Miss Madison," a teacher says to me. "And pick up that paper you just dropped."

Good thing nobody sees what is on my paper. It's another one of them Akeelma letters.

Dear Diary:

When you are hungry, really hungry, even mush crawling with maggots tastes good. So I can't help licking my lips when that girl put the last fingerful of my food in her mouth. A thief, that one is. Yesterday I grabbed her hands and tried to take back what was mine. It fell to the floor, and someone else scooped it up. She is a lion who cares for no one but herself.

—Akeelma

I'm almost to Miss Saunders's room when John-John McIntyre starts up with me again.

"New clothes, huh?" he says, trying to be smart.

I stop walking and turn to him and ask real smart like, "Why you always picking on me?" I ain't sure what's come over me. I guess thinking about Akeelma makes me wonder why people treat others like they're nothing.

"Chill, Maleeka," John-John says, strutting down the hall alongside me. He gets quiet, and I hear his big sneakers squeaking every time they hit the floor.

Then I say something that surprises us both. "Why me?"

He knows what I'm asking. He keeps on stepping.

"Why do you hate me?" I ask, looking right at John-John.

His cheek twitches. "You bugging, girl," he says.

I look at him like he's crazy. John-John's been hating me all my life it seems. Now he's standing here denying it.

"I don't think nothing about you," he says, jerking up his pants.

Seems like nobody's in the halls but me and John-John, only there's plenty of kids around, pushing and shoving one another out of the way. The teachers are trying their best to move all us kids along, but it ain't working so good.

"That song you sing about me ain't right, John-John," I say. "It just ain't right."

"So what? You ain't all that, you know."

All *what*, I want to ask. But John-John don't give me a chance. He says I got what I deserved on the bus that day. He says since the first time he met me, I acted like I was better than him.

I'm looking at John-John like I ain't never seen him before. Better than him? When I do that?

He says something stupid-crazy. Says it was back in second grade when I first moved to the Heights. I walked into class that first day with my new pink polka-dotted dress on and black patent leather shoes. The teacher told me to sit in the desk next to his. I said I didn't want to. I wanted to sit in the one up front, next to Caleb.

"That half-white punk," John-John says, knowing full well Caleb ain't mixed.

Now my mouth's hanging open. "I didn't even know Caleb back then," I say. "I wanted to sit up front, 'cause I couldn't see the board," I explain.

Looking at John-John, I tell him, "You hated me all these years for something I didn't even do."

"No matter," he says. "You given me plenty of reasons not to like you since then. Thinking you super-smart. Acting like you too good for me."

I tell John-John how things really is. "I'm failing all my classes. Char's on my case all the time. I gotta borrow clothes to look like somebody."

"Good," John-John says. "You always thought you was better than me. Now look at you. You just as bad off as the rest of us. Worse, maybe. Caleb don't want no part of you now, I bet." Now John-John's bobbing his head up and down, laughing like this whole thing is funny.

John-John looks at me like I'm dirt or something. I swallow hard. I think about what Daddy once said about not seeing yourself with other people's eyes. I keep on stepping. When I open the door to Miss Saunders's room, John-John's right behind me. For once, Miss Saunders's not getting on my case about being late. Then it hits me. John-John McIntyre is jealous of me. But why?

I sit there for about five minutes trying to figure this thing out with John-John before I notice Miss Saunders ain't here. It's seeing Worm with his narrow butt parked on Daphne's desk that makes me know something's not right. When I look up front, nobody's there but two kids drawing on the board. I guess Miss Saunders is sick. "All right, a substitute," I say. "No work today." Before I can even smile good about it, Miss Saunders comes flying into the room. "Sorry I'm late," she says, all out of breath.

I'm sorry you're here, I whisper.

CHAPTER THIRTEEN

WHY DO TEACHERS TELL YOU STUFF you don't want to hear? Like how wonderful their children are, or how big their house is, or what a quiet, pretty neighborhood they live in. It's Miss Saunders's turn, I guess. She comes in telling us she's late because her toilet ran over and she had to clean her white carpets before they got stained. Like we really care.

She presses her hands against her gray pin-striped pants suit, then pulls the jacket sleeves down. No gold bracelet today, just a watch on one arm and a thin gold necklace around her neck.

Miss Saunders is a motion machine this morning. She sets down her briefcase, throws her black bag into the closet up front, slaps her hands together like giant paddles, and tells everybody to get quiet.

Then she fans herself with her hand. "My landlord had to come over." She's opening and closing drawers looking for who knows what. "I am never late, you guys know that." Now she's fingering the chalk. Pacing the room. There's sweat on her face. She leans herself against the desk and rubs her chin like she's trying to find lost words. "Well, let's get started," she says, not even seeing what we all see up there on the blackboard.

"Who can tell me what Shakespeare meant when he . . . ," she begins, finally getting a good look at our faces.

Everybody is quiet. "Who read the thirty pages I assigned last night?" Miss Saunders asks.

Most of the hands go up, including mine, even though I didn't read none of it.

"Then let's get to work," she says, heading for the blackboard. When Miss Saunders sees what somebody's drawn, she stops in her tracks, like she's been hit in the stomach. There's a woman's face up there on the blackboard. The left side is smooth and pretty. The right side is cracked and drooping like melting wax. It's done in pink, brown and blue. It's a mess, that's all I can say. THE TEACHER WITH TWO FACES. Wiggly words spell it out in blue chalk.

Miss Saunders's big hands erase the board with four quick swipes, like a windshield wiper on full speed. "Who can sum up yesterday's reading for me? John McIntyre?"

She says his name real weird, like maybe she ain't just asking him about schoolwork, but accusing him of drawing the picture. We all stare at John-John. I know he didn't draw the picture. He came into class after me. Miss Saunders carries on with her lesson. "Tell me about today's reading assignment. What would you do if you were Romeo and you loved a girl you couldn't have?"

"Dump her," John-John says, staring right at me. "Why sweat it? There's plenty of girls out there."

Everybody laughs. "John-John, you would not," Carrie Miller says. "If you ever *got* a girl to like you—and we all know that ain't never gonna happen—you'd sell your skin to keep her."

Miss Saunders slaps her hands together to get off the chalk and asks Carrie to hold her thought. Next thing you know, Miss Saunders is sitting on the corner of Carrie's desk, crossing her legs. "Let John tell his story his way. But John, remember. This is the love of your life. Her folks are trying to keep you apart because you're not good enough, so they say."

"Nobody wants to talk about this stuff," I say half under my breath.

Miss Saunders starts, walking the classroom aisles. "What *do* you want to talk about?" she asks us.

"Why Maleeka's so black," John-John says. Miss

Saunders's eyes shoot his way. Her smile is gone and her arms are folded tight.

"Sorry," John-John says, shrugging and folding his arms too.

"Out of my room, John-John." Miss Saunders points to the door.

"But—"

"But nothing," she says.

Man, I'm thinking, why can't she just let it go. Forget about it. Don't she see dragging it out only makes it worse.

Next thing I know, John-John's faking an apology to me, mumbling that he's sorry. "OK, everybody, let's get this thing back on track," Miss Saunders says. "Romeo and Juliet. Give me your thoughts," she says, unbuttoning her suit jacket. "Romeo and Juliet didn't play by the rules. People had expectations for them. Wanted them to act and be a certain way. But they refused."

"Yeah, and they died anyhow," Worm shouts from the back. "So what is your point?"

"*You* tell *me*. Anybody here believe strongly enough to die for something or someone?"

"My homies," Eric yells. "I'd give up blood for one of my boys."

"My momma," shouts Desda.

"Nobody," says Jerimey. "Ain't doing no dying for

nobody but me. It's cold but true. Don't love nobody as much as my own fine black self," he says, kissing his arm from shoulder to fingertip.

Now everybody's cracking up, including Miss Saunders.

"Yeah, Jerimey loves hisself some Jerimey," Raina says.

Jerimey starts rubbing his cheeks. "You gotta love yourself, baby. If you don't, who will?"

"Romeo loved Juliet. My father loves my mother. People love other people," Desda says.

"But when they're gone, who's gonna love you? When Romeo died, Juliet killed her stupid self. She loved him more than her own self. Now do that make sense?" Jerimey says.

Miss Saunders is on the other side of the room now. She's standing right next to Jerimey. "You're saying we shouldn't love people so much?"

"No. I'm saying if you love yourself more than you love me, you will take good care of you. And, you won't try to do me in because that's just gonna cause problems for you. People who love who they are ain't gonna make unnecessary trouble for themselves. Get it?"

"Go ahead, Mr. Philosopher, preach," John-John says, slapping him five.

"Can we get back to Romeo and Juliet?" I say, just to shut him up.

But John-John interrupts again. "You probably didn't even read the book."

"Why you always on Maleeka's case, John-John?" Jerimey asks.

"Shut up," John-John says.

"Make me," Jerimey says, getting out of his seat.

I'm smiling big-time. John-John is getting a taste of some of his own stuff. I like that.

"The period is almost over and you two dingdongs are wasting time," Worm says. Everybody looks at Worm like he's crazy. Since when did *he* care about stuff like Romeo and Juliet?

"Be quiet and let somebody else talk," Carrie says.

"I wish somebody would kill themselves over me," Desda says.

"I'd kill myself if I had to kiss those crusty lips," John-John butts in.

"I mean, ain't that the most romantic thing in the world. Somebody who can't live without you?" Desda goes on, ignoring John-John.

"No," I say before I think about it. "It ain't." I start chewing on my lip, trying to figure my way out of this. But everybody's looking. I keep on talking. "When my daddy died three years ago, Momma fell apart. She couldn't eat. She couldn't sleep. She stayed up all night long, washing and scrubbing till her hands was raw," I say, chewing on my finger.

The class gets so quiet, it's scary. "I was ten years old and brushing her teeth, feeding her oatmeal like a baby. She cried all the time. Last year, she finally came to. Got up one day, went and bought a sewing machine, and started making clothes. Ain't never sewed nothing before. Just started, day and night, sewing."

Some kids at the back of the room start to snicker and make smart remarks. Shut up, I'm thinking. Just shut up.

"The more she sewed them clothes, the better she got. She started picking up after herself. Got a job and all. No, ain't nothing good come from loving somebody so much you can't live without 'em," I say. "No good at all."

Marla asks me why nobody in our family came to help me and Momma out when my daddy died.

I say that we don't have no relatives, but that ain't the truth. Momma's got a sister in New York. Daddy had brothers all over the place. But they weren't close. And getting in touch with them would have meant taking me away or putting Momma in some institution someplace. I wasn't having that, so we lived off Daddy's Social Security and savings.

The classroom gets quiet again. Then the bell rings, busting up the silence like a fist through glass.

CHAPTER FOURTEEN

A FEW DAYS LATER, I'M HANGING out with Char and the twins. Char told me I better show up if I know what's good for me. She says she don't like how I'm acting lately. Forgetting to do her homework. Giving her too much lip. She's right, I'm pushing my luck with her. But maybe I can learn to hang with Char and get along with her too. Fighting her ain't no use. Look where it got me the last time in the lunchroom. I'm tired of working in the school office. It's been a few weeks now, and I'm still bored stiff.

I want to have some fun. So after fifth period, instead of going to the office to work, I head to the lockers with Char, Raina, and Raise. And who do we run into but Miss Saunders, who's on hall duty. The first thing Miss Saunders does is ask me how work is coming in the office.

Then she says, "I guess you're headed there now. You *are* working there today, right?"

Char stays cool, for once, and she and the twins start walking ahead of Miss Saunders and me.

"I'm on my way," I say, turning back around and walking up the hall toward the office.

I hear Miss Saunders tell Char and the twins they better hurry up to class or they will have to get a late note to get in. Char says something smart and keeps stepping. A moment later, I hear the school side exit door closing.

Miss Saunders walks me to the office like I'm some baby. She's dressed to the nines, like usual. She's got on gold hoop earrings with dolphins jumping through them, and she's making small talk. Asking how I am. Asking if I read her latest assignment.

"That a designer suit you wearing?" I ask, knowing full well it is.

Miss Saunders fingers the collar. "I think so."

"You think so. Don't you know?"

"Yes, it is, Maleeka," she says, kind of smart.

"Real teachers can't afford designer suits," I say before I really think about what I'm saying.

"I wore suits for my job at the ad agency. Suits are kind of like a uniform, I guess."

"My mom wears a uniform to work. What you got on *ain't* no uniform."

Miss Saunders nods. I think if I was wearing my own clothes I would feel like two cents next to her. But I'm in Char's stuff, so I'm holding my own.

"What're you doing here, Miss Saunders? At McClenton, I mean?" I ask.

While we walk, Miss Saunders stops every once in a while and picks up a gum wrapper or a soda can tab. "I want to teach," she says plain as day.

"Then, how come you're not at that Catholic school ten blocks from here? Or one of them private schools downtown?"

Miss Saunders doesn't say nothing, she's just walking slow like I got all day.

"I mean, teachers don't come here 'cause they want to. They get dumped here, 'cause they goofed up someplace else, usually. Except Tai, maybe. But you know, she's weird. She wanted to come to McClenton," I tell her.

Then Miss Saunders gives me a trick question that I ain't expecting. "Why are *you* here?"

"What?" I fold my arms tight in front of me.

"Why are you *here?*" she asks again. "I checked your records. Last year you passed the test for Central Middle School, across town."

"You checked my records?"

"I check all my students' records. In business, you always learn about your clients, who they are, what makes them tick. It helps you do your job better. It's the same with teaching—know your clients."

It bothers me that Miss Saunders knows all my business. "You know about us kids. But we don't know nothing 'bout you. Except where you came from before you got here, that you like suits and jewelry, and that you was born with that face."

Miss Saunders says there's nothing much to know about her. She's single. She doesn't have any kids. She was working eighteen-hour days and traveling the country all the time. When she turned forty, she didn't want to do it anymore. Six months later she found out about the school board's new plan for letting executives teach in the schools.

"You gave *that* up to come *here?*" I ask, reaching down and picking up a broken pen.

"The business world can be very competitive," Miss Saunders says. "I was always trying to out-think, out-perform, even out-dress my competitors. It was wearing me down."

"Well, you're the best-dressed one in *this* place," I say.

Miss Saunders reaches for the top button on her suit.

"You think you ever going back, Miss Saunders? Back to working in a big company?" I ask.

Miss Saunders shakes her head. "No, I think teaching is it for me."

"You won't miss the money and stuff like that?"

She shakes her head a second time. We turn the corner and I go into the office. Miss Saunders walks in, throws trash in the garbage can by the door, and keeps on going. It's the first time me and her been together without things falling apart.

CHAPTER FIFTEEN

MISS SAUNDERS HAS REALLY GOT ALL the other teachers stirred up. Except for Tai, most of them don't like her. They say Mr. Pajolli's sucking up to her so that maybe her company will donate lots of money to the school. Maybe even get us some computers and a new library. All of this makes the other teachers resent Miss Saunders even more.

In the office, the teachers never say her name. They just say "she" did this, and "she" did that.

"I hate pushy people," Miss Benson, the English teacher, is saying when she comes into the office with Mr. Pajolli. "Every day, she's coming to me with some new idea she came up with. Questioning why things can't be done differently."

Mr. Pajolli tries to quiet Miss Benson down. But she

just gets louder and her face grows red. Raising her finger to him, she says, "You get her in line, Charles. She's disrupting everything. *Everything.*"

Mr. Pajolli's nodding, while his eyes go over the messages Miss Carol hands him.

"That's the third parent calling to complain this week. Too much homework. Too much reading," Miss Carol says.

A big smile comes over Miss Benson's face. "Don't tell me. Let me guess who they're complaining about."

Mr. Pajolli scratches his bald head. He lets out a deep breath and says he'll take care of things. Then the phone rings.

"Yes, he's here." Miss Carol presses down the hold button and smiles. "Someone else calling about your favorite person."

Mr. Pajolli clicks his false teeth together. "Send it back to my office," he tells Miss Carol.

Miss Benson touches up the edges of her lipstick with her finger and walks off humming. Miss Carol tells me to get back to work and stop being so nosy. I go and staple papers together over in the corner. It's good to see teachers get in as much trouble as kids do sometimes.

The office is a busy place. Folks come and go like this is a bus stop on the corner. As soon as I get a few papers stapled, here comes someone else wanting something. This time, it's Desda.

"Hey, Maleeka. I need me a note to get into class. I been to the dentist," she says, pulling out a balled-up piece of paper with some writing on it.

I look in Miss Carol's direction. She's heading over to give Desda what she needs. While she's doing that, here comes Charlese. I don't see the twins nowhere.

"Charlese, shouldn't you be in class?" Miss Carol asks, still tending to Desda.

"In a minute," Char snaps, waving for me to come to the other end of the counter.

Miss Carol's voice is squeaky and high-pitched like a wheel that needs some oil. "Charlese Jones. I don't know what you think is going on here, but Maleeka is doing a job for the principal. And you, young lady, had better high-tail it to class."

Char just laughs at Miss Carol. "You act like Maleeka is working for the president of the United States. *Man.*"

Miss Carol shoves the note over to Desda. "All right now, get to class."

Desda's looking at me like I did something wrong. Charlese takes out a stick of gum, and pushes it in her mouth real slow. Miss Carol looks like she's going to go off on her. Then out comes Mr. Pajolli.

"Hello, Mr. P.," Char says, in a sweet, baby voice. "You think maybe one day I can work in here, too? Maybe answer the phone or something?"

Char stands there in her skintight striped pants suit with her finger in her mouth like a two-year-old. Mr. Pajolli knows Char ain't the least bit like that for real.

"Sure, Charlese. You may start working in the office as soon as you pay the fines for the three library books and two math books you lost last year."

Char starts arguing with Mr. Pajolli about how she ain't never had those things and how everybody is out to get her. "Anyhow," she says, "I ain't no slave. If I work for somebody, there's got to be some dollars involved."

Mr. Pajolli tells Char to move along, to get to class.

"For what?" she says, heading out. "All these teachers is boring me to death."

Mr. Pajolli asks her what class she has now. "Math, with Tai," Char says.

"Nobody can be bored in her class, unless they want to be," Mr. Pajolli says, walking out with her.

Mr. Pajolli is right, too. Tai *is* funny. She meditates a lot so during her class break it ain't unusual to see her sitting on the desk with her legs folded and her arms crossed.

She's different, but she *can* teach. I used to get all A's in Tai's class last year. Since I got this office gig, Tai's been bugging me about keeping up my average. She came right in here yesterday and asked me where my homework was. Mr. Pajolli was standing right at the desk, too. I lied and said it was in my locker. Tai asked Mr. Pajolli if it was OK for me to go get it. Then I had to fess up and tell her I forgot to do it. She asked Mr. Pajolli if it's OK for me to use my office time to do my math homework. He said, yeah, but that I'd have to make up the time later.

Teachers don't do nothing but cause you grief, I swear that's all they do.

CHAPTER SIXTEEN

YOU GETTING SOFT, MALEEKA, I SAY to myself. It's Saturday morning and I been up two hours already writing this stuff for Miss Saunders. If Char or the twins knew about this, they would think I was out of my mind. Doing schoolwork on the weekend. For fun.

Momma's trying to work me to death today, too. She got me washing windows and clothes and everything else. I tell her I have to do homework. That's the only thing that got me off the hook for now. So here I am, trying to think something up before I head to Char's. It's coming slow, but it's coming.

Dear Diary:
The sea is wild and mean. Water is crashing against the boat like a hundred angry lions. My body is wet

*with sweat and throw-up from the others pressing close
around me like sticks of firewood.*

*They chain us together like thieves and beat us till
we bleed. I have made up my mind, though. I will show
no weakness. I will be strong. Strong like the sea and
the wind.*

—Akeelma

I finish writing, throw the paper in my drawer, and run out
of the house. Momma don't know I'm headed for Char's
place. She wouldn't like it. She says Char's sister, JuJu,
lets Char do anything she wants. Lets her run wild.
Momma's right about that.

Just before I'm about to leave, Sweets calls. She asks
why am I going to Char's if I'm trying to shake Char loose.
"I'm bored," I tell her. "I don't want to go to the avenue or
hang out here at home. Besides, Char asked me to come
over. Her sister's got some new things. I was going to say
no. Then she mentioned something about a black-and-
gold skirt set." I can hear Sweets listening on the other end
of the phone. She doesn't say much before she hangs up.

I thought I would be at Char's by one o'clock. But
Momma keeps finding things for me to do. I have to clean
out the cabinets, sweep, and take clothes to wash at the
laundromat. I swear Momma thinks I'm her slave. She

don't even want to pay me a little something for doing so many chores. She says it's my house, too, and that I should be glad to help.

When four o'clock comes, I'm knocking on Char's door. Can't nobody hear me, though. The music's too loud. Some African stuff is playing. Drums are beating. Singers are making animal noises. Maracas are shaking.

I push open the broken screen door and go inside. JuJu is jamming. Her and about ten other people are dancing. They're rubbing up on one another. When I'm halfway across the room, a man with dreadlocks down to his belt jumps in front of me and says, "Come jam with us, little sister." Then he starts moving like he's a snake. I shake my head and run up the steps. JuJu tells the dreadlocked brother to turn up the music and leave me alone. The music gets louder and so do the pots and sticks people are banging on.

I'm thinking that the party's just got started. But Char says it's finishing up from last night. I ask her how she sleeps through all the noise. She says she ain't been to sleep yet. That she gets paid big bucks from JuJu to keep glasses clean, ash trays emptied, and food coming. "I don't mind missing sleep for a hundred dollars," she says, waving the money in my face.

JuJu parties all the time. Two, three times a month.

People come from all over to go to her parties. Char and I find a place to talk, upstairs, in one of the empty bedrooms. I tell Char I couldn't stand being around so many strangers all the time.

Char says I'm a wimp. That it ain't nothing for her to wake up and find somebody she ain't never seen using her bathroom two days after the party's done. Folks like being around JuJu, she says.

"Don't they work?" I ask.

"Some do, some don't," she says, matter-of-factly. "JuJu don't care as long as they pay to get into the party. She ain't giving nobody nothing for free."

I shake my head. I'm thinking, Ain't no way I could live like this. Cigarette smoke burning your eyes. The house smelling like old chicken grease. Strangers passed out on your living room floor.

None of it bothers Char. As long as she's looking fine, she's all right. But today, she don't look so hot. She's got dark circles under her eyes and her hair is all over her head.

"You look like you've been sleeping already," I say, picking lint out of her hair.

She pushes my hand away. "I caught me a few winks about a hour ago. JuJu didn't even miss me. If she did, I would be in real trouble. She says she don't pay me to sleep."

Then Char lets out a giant yawn. She lays herself

across the bed. I want to tell her I didn't come here to watch her sleep, but I feel sorry for her. So I just sit in the chair, watching her nod off.

But before Charlese can get to sleep good, JuJu yells at the top of her lungs. *"Charlese*, what am I paying you for, girl? Get yourself down here. *Now."*

Charlese jumps up and runs down the stairs.

JuJu's yelling and screaming at her in front of everybody. I keep asking myself, Why is Char taking that from her? Then I remember that Char hasn't got nobody but JuJu. JuJu is only twenty-five.

I sit upstairs by myself for a long while, too scared to go downstairs. Finally, I tell myself to get on outta there. When I do get the courage to go downstairs, it's still a madhouse. Char's running around. People are lined up at the door trying to get in the house. Strangers are asking me where the bathroom is and how come there ain't no toilet paper.

I don't tell Char I'm going. I just walk out the door. Last I seen, Char was rubbing her eyes and handing out drinks. JuJu was shaking her hips and smoking a cigarette, yelling for somebody to turn up the music.

CHAPTER SEVENTEEN

Aₛ ₛₒₒₙ ₐₛ ₜ ᵍₑₜ ₜₒ the street two boys I ain't never seen before start hassling me.

"Hey, bean pole," one of them says.

"You mean, *black* bean," his friend says.

Across the street, some lady yells, "Y'all leave that girl be."

That just makes those boys tease me more. But I ignore them and keep on walking. Soon I'm halfway home. I'm getting hot, so I take my jacket off and sit myself down on some steps to cool off. Most of the houses on the block are vacant. I'm sitting on the curb, imagining what this street would look like if people picked up the trash and gutted some of the buildings. Then, when I look down the street, here come the two boys who were bothering me. I get up and start walking as fast as I can.

I keep putting my finger in my mouth and scraping off nail polish. I cross the street even when I don't have to. They keep coming.

"I like a girl with long legs," one of them says, catching up to me. "A sweet, chocolate brown baby with long legs."

One of the boys is wearing biker pants. He laughs and starts walking faster. I walk fast too.

"Baby, baby, baby," he says, "you my kind of woman." Then he gets in front of me. His friend gets behind me. He's dressed in big, drooping pants that show his underwear.

"Give me a little kiss," he says. "Right here on my soft, juicy lips."

His friend twists my hand behind my back. I yell for him to let me go. But he doesn't.

He's big. He's got muscles in his neck and everywhere else. "Give my friend a little kiss," he says, pushing me toward the other kid.

I tell them to leave me alone. I tell them my dad's a cop and he will lock them up. They don't care. They are having fun.

The boy with the biker pants says that if I just give him a kiss he'll leave me be. "I wanna see what you taste like, is all."

"*No*," I yell. But nobody can hear me. Ain't nothing

alive on this block except mangy cats and stray dogs, and they look like they want to jack me up, too. My heart is beating so fast I can't breathe. "I ain't playing," I say, trying to pull loose from the big one with the droopy pants.

"You pretty black thing," the biker pants kid says. "I ain't gonna hurt you." Then he closes in on me. Tears come running down my face. My head is shaking no. His friend is laughing. Laughing and shoving me closer. I want to scratch his eyes out. Only I can't get my hand loose. Next thing I know, the biker pants guy is standing over me, his breath smelling like green peppers and garlic.

I'm crying. Thinking what to tell Momma. She will be mad at me for walking down a street where nobody lives. I kick the guy who's holding me. He looks like he wants to scream. He lets up on one of my hands for a second while he's yelling for the other kid to hurry up. I dig my fingernails into that other boy's stomach and hang on tight like a crab. He hits me so hard a knot starts to swell on my arm.

Then he puts his hand over my mouth. My heart's about to beat me up inside. I open my mouth, grab hold of his hand with my teeth like a mad dog, and don't let go. He's trying to pull his fingers free. But he can't. He's screaming for me to let him go. But I hang on. He's punching me upside the head, screaming and punching, till finally I set him free.

"You black thing," he says, putting up his big fist like he wants to slam me again. My big teeth marks have left a dent in his hand. He starts loosening his belt with his good hand.

"Forget it, man," the other one says. "She ain't worth it." He shoves me hard. "Next time we see you, you better run," he says.

I don't give those evil kids no second chances. I run like the wind. I run and run and run till I can't breathe no more. When I'm almost home, I sit down on some steps near my house, and cry. My whole body is shaking and seems like it won't ever stop. Tears and snot are running down my face. No more back streets, fool, I tell myself.

When I'm just about home, I run into Sweets. She's headed to the corner store to buy her dad some snuff. I tell her what happened. "Please don't tell Momma," I beg. Sweets agrees. She gives me a sorry look. I know she knows all this happened 'cause I had to be around Char. But she says she'll keep it quiet anyhow.

She gives me a used tissue to wipe my face clean. I don't have no choice but to take the tissue. I can't let Momma see me like this. By the time I get home, I don't look so bad. I tell Momma that some boys was picking on me, but I don't go into no real detail.

Momma studies me for a long minute. "You better be

careful out there," she says, setting a plate of pinto beans, rice, and pork chops down on the table. I rub my sore arm, and try to scoop some beans and rice into my mouth. But my throat won't swallow them down without a struggle.

"I ain't that hungry," I say, leaving the table before Momma can say anything. I go to my room and cry myself to sleep.

CHAPTER EIGHTEEN

Iᴛ's ʙᴇᴇɴ ᴀ ᴍᴏɴᴛʜ ɴᴏᴡ, ᴀɴᴅ all I think about is that thing with those boys. Momma's been saying I got my head in the clouds. She keeps asking if I'm in love or something. I spend a lot of time in my room and don't even talk on the phone, not even to Sweets. Mostly, I'm thinking and writing in my diary—*our* diary, Akeelma's and mine. Lately it's hard to know where Akeelma's thoughts begin and mine end. I mean, I might be starting off with her talking about how scared she is with the smallpox spreading around the ship and killing people. Then I end up the same paragraph with Akeelma saying she's scared that maybe people will always think she's ugly. But I'm really talking about myself. *I'm* scared people will always think *I'm* ugly.

Miss Saunders says it's good that I'm getting so close to Akeelma.

"Good writers get close to their characters," Miss Saunders says.

I've even written in our diary about that thing with the boys, only it ain't *me* the stuff is happening to, it's Akeelma. She's there on the boat, up on deck when the men running the ship come after her.

> *Dear Diary,*
>
> *Where do you run when there's no place to run? They had me trapped. I could see no way out. Then I scratched one on the face, bit the other on his fat, dirty hands. And when I was running, running to hide deep in the crowd up there, I saw someone I knew. It was Kinjari! Kinjari is not dead!*
>
> *—Akeelma*

I showed this last part to Miss Saunders. She said this is powerful stuff. "Writing is clearly one of your gifts, Maleeka," she said. I know it sounds stupid, but when I was leaving Miss Saunders's classroom, I hugged them papers to my chest like they was some boy I've been wanting to press up against for weeks. It feels good doing something not everybody can do.

Momma got a saying: "Don't go getting full of yourself 'cause soon as you do, somebody's gonna come and let the wind out of your sails." Today that somebody is Char. She sees me walking down the hall like I'm wearing clouds for shoes.

"Why you looking all stupid?" she asks, plucking me upside the head. Like a dummy, I tell her about Miss Saunders and my work. Soon as the words are out, I want to kick myself. I said I wasn't telling nobody about this. Now look what I did.

"You Miss Saunders's pet, anyhow," Char says, sticking gum in her mouth. "She got you that job in the office just to keep you away from me, I bet."

I start to tell Char that ain't so, but she don't want to listen. "We're hanging out in the bathroom next period. You coming?" she asks.

"I have to work," I say.

"That's what good little slaves do, obey their masters, right?"

If Char knew, really knew, what girls like Akeelma went through, she wouldn't be talking down slaves.

"You gonna be a slave, or your own master?" Char asks, crossing her arms. If I was my own master, I wouldn't ever speak to you again, I want to say. But, instead, I just tell Char I'll see her later.

"You better be there," she says, walking off. She's halfway down the hall when I hear Worm call her name and see him run to catch up with her. Worm is sliding his arm around Char's shoulder. She yanks it off like he's got body odor. Now that Char has finally stole Worm away from Daphne, she don't even want him no more. That's how she is—sometimey.

It ain't no real choice when you think about it. Hanging with Char and them in the bathroom is more fun than stapling papers in the school office. So when I push open the bathroom door, I put all that stuff about Akeelma and Miss Saunders and the office out of my head. Hanging out in the bathroom is party time, Char likes to say. So I go in there ready to have a good time.

I scoot myself up on the sink and kick off my shoes. Char gets up in the mirror and puts on another coat of mascara. She and the twins, Raise and Raina, laugh. They're talking about Worm and some other boys I don't care nothing about. I smile and act like I'm listening. Next thing I know, I'm reading one of Akeelma's letters.

Char asks what I'm up to. I tell her nothing. She grabs my stuff so hard my books fall on the floor.

"Maleeka's tripping on that slave stuff again," Char says, taking out her cigarette lighter and setting one of my pages on fire. I can feel my ears burning hot with anger. I blow out the burning papers.

"Why does Maleeka got to be with us, anyhow?" Raina asks, putting lipstick on for the third time. "Maleeka is corny and ugly."

Raise sticks her face in the mirror right alongside her sister's. A matching set.

"It used to be fun watching Maleeka half kill herself learning to smoke," Raina says, cutting her eyes at me.

"But Maleeka's just a pain now," says Raise.

Raise and Raina pull back from the mirror at the same time. They both puff up their hair and scratch the same side of their necks at once.

Char says the only reason she lets me hang with her in the first place is to get her grades up.

"It seems like it's been forever, and they ain't up yet," Raina says.

Char shakes her head and smiles. "You're right, Raina. I'm thinking about letting her go anyhow." Char is talking like I ain't even here. "Only I can't cut her loose yet. We got that big book report due in social studies. After that you're history, girl." Now Char is looking my way.

Raina's still on my case. "Maleeka, ever since you got that new hairdo, you think you're something, don't you, Miss Baldy," she says, laughing.

I don't laugh. I look at her like she's getting on my last nerve.

Next thing I know, cigarette smoke is everywhere, and Raise is showing us how to do some new dance. Char asks me to hold her cigarette. She digs in her purse and takes out a marker. She writes her name in big, black letters on the wall near the sink: *Charlese Jones.*

All of sudden, Miss Saunders comes busting into the bathroom, like she's a cop. "All right," she says.

"Dag," Raise says. "Why you always gotta be ruining stuff, Miss Saunders?"

Charlese is pissed. This is the third time Miss Saunders has busted her in the bathroom this month.

Miss Saunders comes over to me and yanks the cigarette out of my hand. "I'm surprised to see you here, Maleeka," she says, flushing the cigarette down the toilet. Then she rubs her hands on her slacks.

"Maleeka ain't no goody two-shoes like you're trying to make her out to be, Miss Saunders," Char says, putting her arm around my shoulder. "Her and me done all kinds of things together."

"Save it, Char," Miss Saunders says, moving up to where I'm standing. She accidentally bumps Charlese's arm and makes her drop her lipstick on the floor. The lipstick lands right on its tip.

"You did that on purpose," Char yells, as she gets up on her toes, up in Miss Saunders's face. But Miss Saunders gets as serious as a heart attack. "I am not a child. I do not play games with children," she says, staring hard at Char.

Char tries to stare down Miss Saunders, only you can tell Miss Saunders ain't backing off.

"That lipstick cost me twenty dollars. It's designer stuff. I want my money," Char says.

When Miss Saunders tells us all to get to the office, there's no mistaking that she means business. She tells everybody to walk a few steps ahead of me and her.

Miss Saunders is harder on me than anybody else. She grabs me by the arm and pulls me off near the lockers. I'm looking at her hand, like she better get off me. I guess she has a second thought about what she's doing, because she turns my arm loose and starts giving me one of her speeches. Talking about how well I was doing in class and working in the office. Telling me I need to choose my friends better.

When we walk into the office, Miss Carol and Maxine act like they haven't even noticed Charlese or the twins. But they have sure noticed me. And I swear I can see the corner of Maxine's mouth go up, like she's holding back a smirk. A teacher standing in the office asks what's happened. Miss Saunders says we were cutting class in the bathroom, smoking, destroying property. Dag, I'm thinking, it wasn't like Char was ripping out the sink. She was just writing her name on the wall with a marker. Just letting people know she'd been there.

CHAPTER NINETEEN

Dear Diary,

They took us up top today. I cried when the sun touched my face. It has been a long time since I seen it. The others, they jumped and ran and laughed like they was free. I sat down in a corner by myself. I stared at the sun, then shut my eyes tight. I want to hold onto the sun for as long as I can. To save up the picture for when I am below again and need to remember that the sun is always shining. I squeeze my eyes closed till I see stars. When I open them again, Kinjari is there.

—Akeelma

The school detention room is in the basement, next to the boiler room. Damp. Cramped. Hot. Nothing but desks and chairs, with Miss Birdy, the detention teacher. Even when it's snowing out, you can go sleeveless in there and still be sweating. Today ain't no different. It's hot. I'm sweating, and it ain't nobody's fault but Miss Saunders's. So here I am, writing in my diary, trying to see the sun.

I'm supposed to be doing English homework. Miss Saunders gave me twenty-five pages to read in two days. I don't get too far with it, though. Caleb comes into the detention room, making noise. He's excusing himself all the way across the room. Squeezing between desks. Knocking over books. You'd think a boy that has been the president of the class and student representative on the PTA would know how to walk into a room.

I'm hoping he will sit up front. No such luck. He plops down two seats away from me, and starts talking before he's seated.

"Hey," he says in that low, soft voice of his.

I stretch my legs out till they're even with the front legs of the chair in front of mine. "What are *you* doing here?" I ask.

"Mr. P. put me in here," he says. "I was doing the boys' bathroom."

For a while, I just doodle on the edges of my paper. But I can't help asking, "Doing what in the boys' room?"

"Scrubbing down the joint," he says plain as day.

"You *cleaned* the boys' room?" I'm frowning up my

face. "You touched the toilet and all that stuff?" Caleb's shaking his head yes with every word I say.

"Disgusting." I suck my teeth.

Miss Birdy comes over to us and tells us to separate. "Get some more space between you," she says. "Two more seats over, Caleb," she insists.

Caleb moves over, then, as soon as Miss Birdy starts grading papers again, he's back near me.

"I don't believe you," I whisper. "Ain't nobody at this school crazy enough to clean the bathrooms," I say, then I shut my mouth.

But Caleb, he does seem crazy sometimes. He and his dad go feed the homeless on the weekends, and once a month Caleb volunteers at the senior citizens home. Last year, he even got the school to hold a neighborhood cleanup day.

"Yeah, I cleaned up the boys' room," Caleb says, smiling. "Got down on my hands and knees like my Momma taught me."

"You should've asked the janitor to help."

"He's doing his job," Caleb says. "It's the rest of us that aren't doing ours."

Caleb's hands don't look like they been in no toilets, even if he was wearing gloves. His hands are big, with nice white straight nails, and his fingers are long and strong and they move all over the place when he gets excited.

Miss Birdy comes over and lectures us about why we're here in detention, and what will happen to us if Caleb doesn't move over and shut up.

For a little while, we write notes to each other.

I write: *Why bother with that smelly bathroom if no one else cares about it?*

Caleb writes back: *You have to take a stand when things aren't right.*

I look at him and wonder why he didn't take a stand last year when we was on the bus, and everybody was making fun of how black I am. Instead of writing back, I open up my folder and start writing in my diary.

Dear Diary:

Caleb smells good. Sometimes when I'm around him, I lose my head. I forget that I am mad at him and that I promised myself I would never, ever forgive him for not coming to my defense on the bus. Those white teeth. Them eyes, and that voice, they make me forget sometimes what he's done. That's why I try to keep away from him. I don't want to forget.

—Maleeka

Caleb looks at me for the longest time. "Things can change," he says. "Like things between me and you, things at the school."

"Don't go there, Caleb," I say.

"I said I was sorry, remember? Said it ten thousand times. Give a brother a break, why don't you?"

"This ain't McDonald's, Caleb. No breaks today," I say, moving to another seat. Caleb's got about six books with him. He takes care of business, keeps up with homework. That's how he is. But even two seats over I can smell him. He don't wear that cheap stuff that hurts your nose like some boys do.

Dear Diary:
    Should you ever forgive a boy who done you wrong?

—Maleeka

Caleb can be persistent. He moves down two seats. Miss Birdy, the teacher, tells us both to settle down, shut up, or be ready to spend the day in detention again tomorrow. That doesn't faze Caleb none. He keeps running off at the mouth.

"Why you bothering me, Caleb?" I ask.

"I shouldn't have left you when they started teasing

you," he says, finally. Then he starts playing with his pencil. Chewing on his lip. We both get quiet for a while. "I figured if I left you, the other kids would stop messing with you."

"How can you think something like that?" I ask.

Caleb says that ever since him and me started hanging together, the kids teased me. So he figured if he got away from me, they'd stop.

"So why you trying to be friends with me again now?" I ask.

He tells me that things are still going bad for me even with him not around, so he figures he can't make my life no worse. "Besides," he whispers, "I still like you . . . a lot."

Eyes don't lie, that's what Akeelma would say. So I look deep into Caleb's eyes. God, they are gorgeous. Big and brown. I think about Akeelma. Right now she'd probably say, "Maleeka, forgive and forget. That's easier than dragging around anger like sacks of stone."

I want to laugh at that one. Those is Momma's words. She says them when I get mad at her. I want to forgive Caleb, but I'm scared. What if I start liking him again and he does what he did before. Momma and Akeelma, *they* could forgive him. I am not that strong at forgiving. Not yet.

Caleb stares at me, all dreamylike. "I didn't mean it, I swear," he says.

"I won't ever let you down again," Caleb says softly.

I nod.

CHAPTER TWENTY

MISS SAUNDERS IS CRAZY. Last week she's got me stuck in in-house detention, this week she's asking me to stay after school so she and me can go over my diary again. I'd promised to meet her as soon as the three-thirty bell rings. I lied. I get to her room at four forty-five. Why should I bust my butt getting to her when she got me put in in-house detention?

Instead of rushing, I stay and help Miss Carol do some Xeroxing, then watch the cheerleaders rehearse outside. When I get to Miss Saunders's room, she's not even there. The janitor says she's in the auditorium. We have to give speeches in her class tomorrow and she wants us to each do it from the stage in front of a mike. She's there checking out the equipment.

I figure Miss Saunders is on the stage, so I go into the

auditorium by the backstage. The ninth graders are putting on *The Wiz* and they got all kinds of junk on stage. I hit my toe on a wooden monkey, and almost trip over some long ropes and cables. I want to scream when I see the witch's costume hanging on a hook in the corner like somebody's in it.

I can overhear Tai and Miss Saunders talking. They can't see me where I am. "This stuff was supposed to be off the stage for my class tomorrow," Miss Saunders is saying. "Nobody here does what they say they will, when they say they will. Thanks for agreeing to help me move it, Tai."

Tai stands up and walks over to Miss Saunders. They push two tables toward the stage curtains, then stop to take a breath. "I don't mind. I like the kinds of things you're doing to keep students interested," Tai says.

I start to leave backstage when something Miss Saunders says makes me stop in my tracks. "I wish it was helping their grades, though. Half my seventh graders are flunking this semester."

Tai's eyes look like they gonna fall out of her head. Mine probably do, too. "How can that be?" Tai says, standing and stretching her arms to the ceiling. Then, bending over like a ballerina taking a bow, she grabs hold of her ankles and pulls her head in between them. "I hear your students in class. They love it. They get so excited."

Miss Saunders bends over to get a good look at Tai. "They are so enthused in class. Full of great ideas."

"That's great," Tai says, standing and stretching from side to side.

"Their insights are fantastic," Miss Saunders says. "Right on target. But their test-taking skills are just terrible."

Tai heads for the bed Dorothy wakes up in when she finally makes it home, and grabs one end and starts talking. "That's not unusual for many of our kids. But you've managed to get them to like Shakespeare. To read something other than the *TV Guide*. Help them learn to test better. Don't kill their spirits by flunking them and making them think that nothing they've done really counts."

Miss Saunders sits down on the edge of the bed. "I can't give them what they haven't earned."

"Nobody is asking you to do that," Tai says.

Miss Saunders says McClenton students have to be held to the same standards as other kids around the city. Tai says that's true, but that tests ain't the only way to prove you know something.

"They will thank me later," Miss Saunders says.

Tai sits down on the bed and folds her legs. "If you're still here."

Miss Saunders stands and folds her arms tight.

"I know the students have been hard on you. The picture on the blackboard. The name-calling in the halls. Kids telling you to buy a new face."

"I don't want to talk about it. Let's get this stuff off-stage." Miss Saunders gets up and starts dragging the end of the bed toward where I'm standing backstage. I'm fumbling with my book bag and trying to get out of there. But I don't make it too far. I can't help wanting to hear what they're saying.

Tai walks over to the edge of the stage and sits down. Her short legs look funny hanging over the side. She starts drawing circles on the floor with her fingers. "Ease up," she says to Miss Saunders. "None of us is perfect."

"That's easy for you to say," Miss Saunders says. Then she starts talking real soft and sad. Telling Tai how when she was little, she prayed to God to make her face perfect. "He didn't," she says, "so I tried to make up for it. To be perfect at everything else I did."

Then Miss Saunders says she always had to be better than everyone else at everything, because people always thought she was less-than due to her face. She says she's always had to dress better. To get the highest grades and be the most creative. At her job, she had the highest sales record in the company for six years straight. "Even here at McClenton," she says, "I put in longer hours and give students an educational experience that they won't find anywhere else."

"That's a lot of pressure to put on yourself and everyone else," Tai says, coming closer to Miss Saunders. "You are a great teacher, with good ideas. These kids will like you no matter what you look like," she says. "But it's your need to be perfect that will ruin you here, not how you look."

Miss Saunders takes out a mirror and starts redoing her lipstick. The next thing I know, she's staring right at me through that mirror. "Maleeka Madison, you little sneak."

CHAPTER TWENTY-ONE

IF IT WASN'T FOR TAI, I don't know what Miss Saunders would have done to me. Even from where I'm standing backstage, I can see that she's pissed. Teachers don't go for you knowing their personal business. That's the one thing besides hitting them that makes them go totally nuts.

All that yoga and kung fu stuff Tai does must really work because she's calm. Real chilled out. Miss Saunders is fidgeting. She is sitting there with her arms crossed.

Tai asks me to have a seat. Then she explains how it's not polite to listen in on other people's conversations. I know she's right. I tell her I won't repeat nothing I heard. Tai believes me, but Miss Saunders, she just ain't buying it.

I didn't tell Char nothing about the incident when I saw her the next day. Char is one of the kids flunking English, so I know hearing some dirt on Miss Saunders would make her day. But I keep quiet about it. Besides, Miss Saunders is gonna get hers soon enough. Char told JuJu she was flunking English and it's because Miss Saunders don't like her. Char says JuJu told her not to worry. JuJu says she'll handle things.

In class Miss Saunders says she wants to see me after school. It seems that woman don't know how to make nothing happen during the school day. She always makes you stick around later for her.

After school when I walk into Miss Saunders's classroom, she's got her feet on the desk and her head shoved all up in a book. When she sees me, she takes her feet down off the desk.

"Good. You came," she says. "Sit, sit down."

I sit down and hope she's gonna make it quick.

Miss Saunders is suited-down and buttoned-up tight, like usual. Today she's got on a blue suit with gold buttons, the same kind they got on navy uniforms.

"I wanted to speak with you, Maleeka." Miss Saunders starts rubbing her hands together, cracking her knuckles. "About your diary. We never did discuss it. How is it coming along?"

Before she says anything else, I pull out papers and show her my stuff. I'm talking to her about Akeelma, like Akeelma's a real person.

Miss Saunders says my stuff is good. She tells me I get *two* A's for it. Says I can keep it up if I want to, but she won't make me. I look her up and down. I tell her I don't know what I'm gonna do. I ain't for doing schoolwork when I don't have to.

Miss Saunders gets real quiet. She acts like she doesn't want me to leave. I'm missing the "I Love Lucy" show on account of her, so I stand up to go. She finally gets around to what she's been wanting to say all along, I guess. "Have you told anyone about my conversation with Tai?" Miss Saunders gives me a hard look and goes on about how important it is for a teacher to not have her personal business out among students. How it can "undermine her credibility," whatever that means.

"Well, you don't need to worry," I say, coming closer to Miss Saunders's desk, "I ain't telling." Some teachers got pictures of their family on their desks. Their kids, husbands, even their dogs. Tai, she got pictures of this little Korean girl she sends money to every month. Miss Saunders ain't got nothing or nobody on hers. It's like she ain't got no life except for her life at work.

Miss Saunders gets up, and paces the room. She don't know what to say next. I can tell. All this walking around she's doing is starting to get to me. I go to the blackboard and start drawing on it. "You act like you're the only one in the world who's been teased," I say, looking her right in the eyes. "Please. Look at me."

Miss Saunders stiffens up.

I keep talking. "Some of us is the wrong color. Some is the wrong size or got the wrong face. But that don't make us wrong people, now does it?" I sit myself on my desk and put my feet up, like Miss Saunders had done. "Shoot, I know I got my good points, too."

Miss Saunders cracks a smile. "Maleeka, you have a lot of good points," she says. Then she says how good I am at writing and math. And she starts in on me about bringing up my grades.

Before she gets too far, I ask, "You got any friends?"

Miss Saunders hunches her shoulders. "I've had a few in my time. It's hard to keep them, with all the traveling I did in my corporate job."

"Tai and you are buddies, right?"

"Girl, you ask a thousand questions," Miss Saunders says. Then she answers me straight. "Yeah, Tai and I have been friends since college. Tai was the one that suggested I come here to McClenton."

I gather my books and prepare to leave. "I'm glad you've got *one* friend," I say.

CHAPTER TWENTY-TWO

I'M ALMOST HOME BEFORE I REMEMBER that I want to enter my writing in a library contest. So I turn around, walk back to the library, and talk to the librarian. She says the contest winner will get one hundred dollars. I sign myself up right away. I tell the librarian I'm gonna turn my papers in tomorrow.

At home after I eat, I go straight to my room and rewrite all of Akeelma's stuff. I write them up real nice and neat. When I'm finished, I only have five pages. That ain't enough, I'm thinking. So I stay up half the night writing more. Momma comes to my room a few times and tells me to go to bed. But I beg her to let me stay up till I finish.

Dear Diary:

Kinjari isn't so skinny anymore. They had him working the crew, so they let him eat good. I cried when I saw him. I curled up in a ball and hid my face. Kinjari came closer, and sat next to me. "There is no one more beautiful than you, Akeelma," he said. That only made me cry more.

"I'll go where you go," he said in my ear.

"You were a good boatbuilder at home," I said. "They will want to keep you here when the ship docks. You will be free, almost."

Kinjari told me that he could never work on a boat like this just to see the sun and feel the wind whenever he pleased. "I would rather be a slave with you than be free by myself," he said.

Then he held my chin and helped me drink water from a wooden cup. At first I would not look him in the eyes. But then when I did, I was glad. Kinjari's eyes warmed me like the sun.

—Akeelma

I never talked to Momma about Akeelma till last night. When I got up this morning, she asks how things turned out. I let her read my diary page.

"You're a good writer," Momma says, setting the

papers down gently. "You could be a professional writer someday," Momma continues, sounding just like Miss Saunders. "Like your father."

"Daddy wrote stuff? Stuff like this?" I ask, putting my hand down on the papers.

"He wasn't as good as you," Momma says, going to the sink for a glass of water. She won't drink cold water from the fridge, just warm tap water. "But your father, he wrote nice letters, poems, stuff like that."

"He ever write a poem about you—or me?" I ask.

"Don't you remember the poem he wrote about you? The one about you being beautiful?" Momma asks.

"Me? What?" I ask, getting excited. "No, I don't remember. When did Daddy write that. Where is it?"

"I don't remember," Momma says, getting up for more water. Then she stops in her tracks. "Well, now, let's see," she says, scratching her head. "Maybe it's in that box in my closet. I put stuff there that your dad gave me. I forgot about the poem, though, till just now."

I run up the stairs, two at a time. I hop over the top step and almost fall into Momma's room. I push past the shoe boxes full of dream books and no-good lottery tickets and fabric scraps, and go for the one marked with my dad's name—*Gregory*. I lift the box out of the closet like a fragile piece of glass. But I'm too scared to open it up. When I do, tears come to my eyes. There's pictures of me and Daddy standing in front of the house. Playing football in the yard. Him carrying me on his back up the stairs. I haven't seen these pictures since Daddy died.

Momma's yelling for me to hurry up because I got to go to school in a half hour. I'm looking through all the pictures but I don't see no poems. I find Daddy's birth certificate and the driver's license from when he drove a cab. I just about give up, but then I see a crumpled brown paper bag that's been smoothed out and folded tight. The words is written out real neat and straight and strong.

Brown
Beautiful
Brilliant
My my Maleeka
is
Brown
Beautiful
Brilliant
Mine

Momma is calling me. I can't answer. My mouth is full of Daddy's words, and my head is remembering him again.

Tall, dark, and smiling all the time. Then gone when his cab crashed into that big old bread truck. Gone away from me for good, till now.

"Maleeka, you got to go to school, girl," Momma says, heading upstairs.

I fold the poem and stuff it in my pocket. Then I take the picture of Daddy with me on his back and put that in my other pocket.

"Find anything?" Momma asks, sitting next to me on the bed.

"Just some stuff," I say, walking out of the room to get my jacket.

Momma doesn't ask what kind of stuff. It ain't that she don't care. She just ain't ready to look or listen to Daddy again. She shoves the pictures back in the box, and puts the box on the shelf. I kiss Momma good-bye, and soon she's in the sewing room, threading the needle. By the time I shut the front door, all I hear is that sewing machine going like crazy.

CHAPTER TWENTY-THREE

AT SCHOOL I SKIP LUNCH PERIOD, and go over to the library and hand in my stuff for the contest. The librarian says that over one hundred kids have entered this contest. I almost take back my entry when she tells me that. But then I start thinking about how much time I put into my writing. I ain't got nothing to lose, I tell myself. I'm almost out the door when I see some books on the table. They're poetry books, so I sit down and look at them for a while, and think about Daddy all over again.

Working in the principal's office has got its benefits. You get to see and hear everything. Like parents coming in to tell Mr. Pajolli off. JuJu came by today. She didn't have an appointment. But she wouldn't leave, so they pulled Miss Saunders out of class and got somebody else to cover her for a while.

Before Miss Carol can open her mouth to speak, JuJu is screaming loud as anything. She's saying her sister is failing because of Miss Saunders.

Mr. Pajolli comes rushing out of his office, asking JuJu to quiet down. He puts out his hand, and introduces himself. JuJu looks at his hand like dirt's on it. She ain't gonna shake it. He asks her to calm down. She won't.

JuJu starts saying who she is and what she's come for. She's got on a skintight, fire-engine-red dress that swishes like cheddar cheese on a grater every time she moves.

She's banging her fist like a gavel on the front desk. She sticks her long, bony finger in Mr. Pajolli's face and says, "Before that woman came, Char got A's. Now, all she gets is D's. What's up with that?" she shouts.

JuJu's right about Char's bad grades. As soon as Miss Saunders came here, she separated me and Char's seats. I guess she could see I was letting Char cheat off me. I ain't been doing Char's homework like I was, neither. Lately, I been making up excuses, saying Momma's keeping me busy with chores, stuff like that.

Before Mr. Pajolli answers JuJu, JuJu is on to a new subject. "Char's all the time talking about that woman at home. Mostly how mean she is. And ugly. That teacher can't be taking her problems out on my sister just 'cause she got burnt on the face or something."

Mr. Pajolli asks JuJu to come into his office. "No," JuJu says. She's not leaving until she sees Miss Saunders. Mr. Pajolli finally tells Miss Carol to send for Miss Saunders.

Miss Saunders comes into the office with her head up and her grade book under her arm. She's wearing red today, too. She seems calm, maybe because she's never met JuJu before.

Mr. Pajolli waves his hand for JuJu to follow him to the office. JuJu shakes her head. "No. We ain't hiding this behind no closed doors. I want this thing out in the open. Right is right, so let's handle our business here," JuJu says.

Mr. Pajolli stands his ground. "Business is handled in my office or not at all."

JuJu's still mouthing off but she follows behind Mr. Pajolli. "This is Char's third time in seventh grade," she's saying. "Char can't afford to do no more time here. Her other teachers know that. They're giving her the grades she needs to move up."

Miss Saunders hands JuJu some papers. Most of them are incomplete, she says. Charlese would rather pass notes than do assignments, Miss Saunders tells her. JuJu eyes the papers.

I don't know what happened next. Miss Carol told me to go get the janitor and tell him the principal wants him to clean up the mess in the boys' room. Miss Carol could have called the janitor on the intercom. She wanted to get rid of me, is all. The next time I see JuJu, she's stomping out of the office, saying Char better not flunk seventh grade. Her feet sound more like bowling balls falling to the ground than feet. Then all of a sudden she stops and stares Miss Saunders up and down. "You don't know what you're doing. You never even taught kids before. You flunk my sister, you won't teach nowhere else. I know people. Big-time people," she says, walking out of there.

CHAPTER TWENTY-FOUR

MISS SAUNDERS DOESN'T KNOW what she did, pissing off Charlese and JuJu. Now, all Char does is talk about getting back at Miss Saunders. She ain't joking, neither.

Last year when the gym teacher flunked her, Char ripped a hole in the top of her convertible. Hot-glued another teacher's grade book together when he told her sister she was missing too much class.

Me and Char and the twins are hanging out behind the school when Char says Miss Saunders is gonna get it the worst, that we're gonna meet tomorrow at school at the crack of dawn to start messing up Miss Saunders. I'm watching the sky. Lightning is flashing across it like God is trying out his electricity. And the clouds are black, like rain's gonna pour any minute.

I'm scared of storms. Char ain't. She loves watching

rain beat on people and lightning chase people inside. "We gonna jack Miss Saunders up," she says, putting another coat of blueberry grape polish on her nails. "I hate that ugly woman. Hate her."

I think about telling Char about the conversation I heard between Miss Saunders and Tai in the auditorium, but I don't. I ain't no squealer. Never was, never will be.

"Give me five," Raina says, walking over to Char, ignoring me. "What's shaking?"

Char tells Raina how she's gonna get even with Miss Saunders. "It's payback time," Char says, laughing out loud.

I ignore them and keep watching the sky.

"You know that big globe Miss Saunders got in her room? The one she says cost all that money. Well, that's gonna be the first to go," Char says. "Gonna carve that sucker in two like a Thanksgiving turkey."

Raina and Raise slap each other five and talk about spray painting the walls.

"You gonna do all that, just because you got in-house detention?" I ask. Char and the twins turn away from me. I swallow hard. "You been on detention before, Char. Why you getting all crazy now?" I ask.

Char keeps polishing her nails. "Ain't nobody ugly as Miss Saunders gonna be embarrassing me every time I turn around. Then go ragging on me to my sister JuJu.

I can't just let that go. Just wait. Tomorrow morning's just the beginning."

"I can't get in no more trouble with Miss Saunders," I whisper.

"Shut up, Maleeka," Raise says. "Char knows what she's doing."

"I sure do," Char says, throwing her nail polish at my head. The bottle misses me, but breaks open on the steps.

"I can't get in no more trouble. That's all I know," I whisper.

If things ain't bad enough already, here comes John-John McIntyre and his crew. "The sky's gonna be as black as you in a minute, Maleeka," he says, looking up at the clouds. His friends think he's funny. They laugh and give a few high fives. Then they start singing, "Maleeka, Maleeka, we sure wanna keep her. . . ."

"Shut up," Char yells. "John-John McIntyre, I will kick your butt," she says, going after John-John.

"Jack up Char," one of his friends says. "Who she think she is coming at you that way?"

John-John don't say nothing. He just looks at Char with a stupid smirk on his face.

"See you later, Midnight," he says to me.

I can feel myself getting mad, my fists balling up at my sides.

Then I remember a poem about midnight that I seen in one of those poetry books at the library. The words of the poem come tumbling in my head, and I start to smile.

Midnight

At midnight, if you have eyes to see,
There's beauty and there's majesty.

Sweet brown babies tucked in tight,
Shooting stars bursting through the night.

Strong, sturdy trees reaching for the sky
Dancing and swaying to the moon's lullaby.

Quiet waters. Silent nights.
Angels soaring toward the light.

At midnight, if you have eyes to see
There's beauty and there's majesty.

Char don't understand what's going on with me. She looks at me and calls me stupid, the way I'm smiling to myself. Then she tells John-John to shut his big, stupid mouth.

He winks and keeps moving. But he's still looking back at me, like he can't figure out what's got a hold of me.

Char's saying something about how she's gotta always look out for me, but I ain't listening really. I'm saying that poem over in my head again and again.

Next thing I know, here comes Caleb. When Char sees him, she starts talking real proper, all up in his face, telling him how she likes his braids. Asking the name of that cologne he's wearing.

"Hey, Maleeka," he calls to me, ignoring Char. Caleb sure looks good. And he smells even better. He's got on a lime-green African dashiki with tiny golden swirls stitched on it. He and me just stand there, smiling at each other.

Char pushes herself between us. "You can thank me for how good Maleeka looked," she says, snuggling up to Caleb. "I bought them clothes for her. Gotta keep my girl looking good," she says, licking her lips.

Caleb tries to peel Char's fingers off his arms. It ain't easy, she's holding on tight. "I've been thinking some more about what we talked about in detention," Caleb says to me, finally getting Char off him and moving closer to where I am. "I been thinking about changing things around here. Making things better," he says.

"What you mean, like scrubbing floors?" I ask, wrinkling my nose.

"Some of us are getting together tomorrow to talk about ways to improve McClenton. You should come, Maleeka," he says, peeling Char's hand off him again.

"Maleeka's busy," Char snaps.

"Yeah," I say. "Busy."

"Come after you're done then," Caleb says.

Char busts out laughing. "Sure, Maleeka will come after she's done. Me, too. I'm coming, too. We're *all* gonna help save the school, right, Maleeka?" she says, shoving me so hard I almost fall down.

I'm half listening. I'm trying to figure a way out of this mess. Ever since Char came up with this plan of ruining Miss Saunders, I been praying for God to give me a strong spirit like Akeelma's and Kinjari's.

"Listen up, Maleeka," Caleb says, grabbing hold of my arm, and whispering in my ear. "Your girl Char is whacked. You better stay clear of her before she ends up taking you down with her."

"Char and me are friends," I say quietly.

"Yeah, right," Caleb says, shaking his head. "Char's the kind of friend that will get you locked up or shot up," he says, walking away.

When Caleb is all the way down the street, I can still smell his cologne. I can still hear him warning me to stay clear of Char. He don't know what he's saying, though.

You can't just stop being Char's friend. She don't go for nothing like that.

"Maleeka, get over here." Char's screaming at the top of her lungs, like I'm far away.

My heart starts beating fast and wild. I know Char's plan ain't gonna mean nothing but trouble for me. But I got to go along, anyhow. Nobody ever turns their back on Char. Not unless they're tired of living or something stupid like that.

CHAPTER TWENTY-FIVE

I **LAY AWAKE IN BED** three whole hours before I sneak out of the house to meet Char. I keep trying to think of some reason I can give Char for not showing up. A good reason that Char will buy, so I won't get my butt kicked. But I'm too scared to think straight, so I put on my clothes and go.

It's still kind of dark when I get to school. During school hours, the front door is locked and kids have to be buzzed in. But early in the morning like this, when the janitors and the folks who do the cooking are just making their way in, the door is unlocked.

We all meet by the side of the building and make sure it's clear before we go in. I'm trying to tell Char I don't think I want to do this, but she ain't listening. She's telling me to be quiet and to get going inside.

Raina, as stupid as she is, lets the door slam shut behind us.

"Who's there?" the janitor yells from one of the classrooms.

We don't move. All four of us stand there like dummies ready to be caught. Lucky for us, the janitor ain't much worried. He doesn't bother to come and see what's the matter. He just turns up his portable radio, and starts singing.

We laugh and tiptoe down the hallway right past the classroom where he is cleaning. Maybe this won't be so bad, I think. Then we run up the steps, Char's high heels sounding like hammers banging nails whenever she takes a step.

You would think Miss Saunders would lock up her room like the other teachers do. But she doesn't. She told us once that this was our school, and we needed to take responsibility for it. That if things got destroyed, it was us that missed out, not nobody else.

Miss Saunders has redone her classroom, like she does for every new book we take on. Monday, we start *Ali Baba and the Forty Thieves*.

Her classroom has got about a hundred ribbons hanging from the ceiling. Sheer puffy curtains are tacked to the walls. The room is full of purples, pinks, and greens.

All them colors and curtains make the room look soft and safe.

Our desks are pushed up against the back wall, and lots of pillows, like they sit on in them Arabian movies, are scattered all over the place. Char throws herself down on the pillows and stretches out like she's gonna be here awhile.

"Maybe we should go," I say. "Miss Saunders has just done the room over. She's gonna kill us for messing it up."

Char rolls her eyes my way. "Payback has got to cost something," she says, laughing.

I take a long, deep breath and look down at my clothes. I'm wearing the ones Momma made. Char's got a bag in her hand with the clothes she's gonna give me today. I want to tell her to keep the stuff. But I keep my mouth shut and take the bag.

The twins are the first to go into Miss Saunders's desk. Raise grabs a bottle of glue and swirls a design on a red velvet pillow. Then she takes the gooey pillow and smears it cross the windows and walls.

Char lets out a low, mean laugh, and reaches up and yanks some curtains down. She tells Raise to hand her the scissors, then she jabs holes in the curtains. Raise and Raina stab the pillows, pull out the stuffing, and toss the feathers around the room.

Nobody notices me for a long while. I'm standing by the door staring till Char says, "Get over here, Maleeka. You're in on this too."

I have to do something. They'll think I'm chicken if I don't. So I get Miss Saunders's grade book out of the desk. Her watch is sitting there ticking loud as a clock. I close the drawer and erase a bunch of D's in the book. I put A's in their place.

"Is that it, Maleeka?" Char says. "You gotta do better than that. Get over here." She takes a lighter out of her pocket and hands it to me. She tells me to burn the pile of money on the table. It's not the kind of money we use in this country. It's some foreign money, with puffy-headed kings and queens wearing tall collars.

"I want all that money gone," Char says, heading back for the desk and digging around inside.

I don't move. I stand real still.

"You hear me talking?" Char asks. She digs around in the desk drawer, shoves something in her pocket, and dumps the drawer on the floor.

"This ain't right," I whisper.

Char grabs hold of my hand, and says, "Do it, or I ain't never gonna bring you no clothes."

I shake my head. "No."

"You protecting Miss Saunders?" Char wants to know.

"You protecting that hussy? Why? She don't like you, neither. All the time making a fool out of you in class. You stupid girl. Do like I say or I'll do something to mess *you* up."

I don't say nothing. Even though Miss Saunders and I didn't hit it off right away, she is still a teacher, I tell Char. She still runs the show.

Char grabs hold of my shoulder blade and squeezes till my knees get weak. "Like I said, I will jack you up, girl. Do you hear me?"

While Char's pinching my shoulder, she takes her baby finger and sticks it up her nose like a plug in a sink. She blows hard, sending a bunch of snot splattering over the money. "Do what I say or I'm gonna do worse yet," she says, flicking her lighter's flame close to my head.

I stare Char in the eyes. Momma always says you can tell a person by their eyes. Char's eyes don't have no life to them. They're cold and hard like flat black skipping rocks you find at the bottom of the creek.

I shake my head. "No, I ain't doing it," I say softly. But Char squeezes my shoulder so hard, I hear my bones creak.

I grab the lighter with my other hand and set the money on fire. The kings and queens curl up, turn black, and disappear. There's nothing but ashes on the table.

Char lets me loose, and heads over to the twins. I'm crying in the corner, wishing I could undo this whole school year. Wishing I could go back to being who I was, not somebody's fool.

I'm rubbing my arm when I hear something popping and sizzling. It's the curtains on the wall—they're on fire!

"Girl, you in trouble now," Char says to me, her eyes wide.

"Shhh," Raise says, peeking out the door. "Somebody's out there. It's the janitor. He's around the corner, heading our way."

"I'm outta here," Char says.

She's the first to run. I'm the last. I'm grabbing hold of the bag of clothes she brought me. When I pick it up, the bag rips and the clothes fall out. I'm shoving them back in and trying to run at the same time. Clothes are dropping with every step I take. The janitor is yelling my name. "Maleeka, Maleeka Madison. What you doing here? . . . Oh my Lord. . . . What have you done, girl?"

I run down the steps, two at a time. I fall down and bust open my knee. When I'm out of the building, Char and the twins ain't nowhere in sight. It's just me out there and fire engines from the stationhouse around the corner coming to undo what I just done. Rain is coming down and plucking me on the head. I look left, then right, and finally run home, crying my eyes out.

CHAPTER TWENTY-SIX

I CAN HARDLY GET THE KEY in the lock. My hands are shaking. Shaking like crazy. I hold the key with my steady hand, but I still drop it. Miss Jackson, our neighbor, has a bunch of dogs that are barking like mad. Growling like they wanna come tear me to pieces. *Where's that key?* I scream in my head. My knee is still bleeding, while I'm crawling around looking for the key.

When Miss Jackson sticks her head out the window, shushing them dogs, I keep real still. Still as stone. Miss Jackson's looking to see why her dogs are so excited. She misses seeing me and slams her window shut.

Them dogs know I'm here, though. They start barking again. Jumping against the fence like they're trying to knock it down and come for me. Them dogs would eat you alive if they could.

I finally find the key, but then I drop it again. How am I gonna explain this to Momma, tell her I set fire to a classroom?

Finally, I let myself inside. I take off my shoes. Put them near the couch. Then head upstairs … real slow. But them old wooden steps, they talk. Every time I set foot on one, it tells on me. They creak like crazy. So I step real soft. I put my foot down easy as a baby going down for a nap. I get three steps out of the way. *Four. Five.* Momma is still snoring. *Nine.* I hear Momma turning over. Talking in her sleep. *Ten, the last step. Almost home free.*

My heart is beating hard. My breath is coming out of me like I just run ten blocks.

The last step is the worse. It creaks the loudest. I walk right on past Momma's room. Then the phone rings. Rings louder than I ever heard before. And here I am, standing in the hall, right next to Momma's bedroom.

I hurry up and get in my room. I grab hold of the phone and peel off my clothes at the same time.

"Your momma up, girl?" Miss Jackson says.

Oh my God, I think, kicking my clothes under the bed. Big-mouth Jackson seen everything.

"No, Miss Jackson, Momma's knocked out asleep. Better call back later," I say.

Momma comes out of nowhere. "How am I gonna

sleep with all this racket," she says, scaring me so bad I almost drop the phone.

I swallow hard.

"Is that phone for me?"

Momma grabs the phone and starts fussing with Miss Jackson. Miss Jackson can't hear too good, so Momma is yelling. It sounds like Momma promised to take her to the doctor on her day off tomorrow. Miss Jackson's got the wrong day, and wants Momma to take her this morning. But Momma tells her she's working today. They start to argue. Momma's talking to me and Miss Jackson at the same time.

"Turn over and go back to sleep," Momma says to me, fixing my covers.

I turn over and promise God that if he gets me out of this mess I will never do anything like this again.

Momma starts to say something else to me, but she's too busy arguing with Miss Jackson.

CHAPTER TWENTY-SEVEN

MOMMA **FOUND OUT WHAT I DONE.** I ain't never gonna get off punishment. That's what Momma says. She whopped me all the way from the school security guard's office to our house. I got suspended at school. Every time Momma thought about that, she whopped me again. I was so embarrassed.

Momma never hit me before, not till today. Momma can't hardly talk or look at me. She's been crying all day. She doesn't even go to work, play the numbers, or look at the stocks. She just talks to the neighbors and cries. I stay upstairs as long as I can. When my stomach starts hurting, I head downstairs to get something to eat.

"You want some of my tea?" Momma asks. "I didn't drink it yet." She pushes her cup over to me, and sits there a while, rubbing my hands with her warm, soft fingers. We both start crying.

"I didn't mean for it to happen, Momma," I say.

"Shhh," she says. Then she comes over to me and holds me in her arms and rocks me like she did when I was little. "Maleeka, I been thinking all day how to undo what you done. How to pay the school back. How to get you to tell me who put you up to this. Look at my arms," she says, rolling up her dress sleeves. They're covered with tiny red bumps. So is her neck and one of her ears. Tiny bumps break out on every part of Momma's body when her nerves get the best of her. Most times, I put lotion on them to make them stop itching.

"I been thinking all day. Trying to figure out how to raise two thousand dollars to pay for the damages. The more I thought about it, the more I broke out in bumps," she says, scratching. Then, she goes on. She talks so calm and peaceful. She says she realizes that I'm not gonna learn nothing from her trying to save me. "You gotta think that you worth saving, baby. Gotta realize that who you are is all you got."

Momma says that she believes that someone as smart as me can figure her way out of this mess, no matter how big it is. Me, I'm scared to death. I'm begging Momma not to do this to me. I'm crying, wiping snot and tears away. I'm following Momma out of the kitchen, asking her to talk to the teachers and make this thing right again. But Momma ain't having it. She turns on the hallway light and heads upstairs.

I try not to cry, but I can't help it. Momma ain't being

fair. I want to remind her that when Daddy died, *I* was there for *her*. How come she can't be here for me now? But when Momma makes up her mind, there ain't no use in trying to change it. Two thousand dollars. She knows I can't get money like that.

I'm thinking about how I can make me some money. But before I can think on it too much, the phone rings. It's Charlese. She wants to know if I told on her. "No," I say, "but that don't mean I ain't gonna."

"Maleeka, hang up that phone. You know you on restriction," Momma says, from the bathroom.

"All right, Momma," I call, acting like I'm hanging up. I lower my voice and tell Char I got to go. But she keeps on talking.

"I can't get in no more trouble," she says. "Last time I cut the roof on that teacher's car, they said I would be expelled from school if I did anything like that again."

"Well, I'm already suspended," I say. "Why should I get in trouble by myself? I said we should leave the school. Why didn't you listen?" I say. What I want to tell Char is, so what if she gets kicked out of school. She's too old for seventh grade anyhow. But I don't say nothing. Char's sister JuJu is gonna pay her four hundred dollars if she gets herself through seventh grade this time. Char don't want to lose that kind of cash. No way.

Char admits that she should have listened to me, but it's too late now. She just wants to know if she can count on me keeping my mouth shut. If I do, she says, she will bring me even better clothes to wear.

I don't know what to do. Ain't no need for all of us to get in trouble. Bad enough I got caught. "Y'all gonna help me pay this money back?" I ask.

"Yeah. We got your back, girlfriend," Char says. Then, "So you won't tell? We in the clear? The twins and me?" she asks before she hangs up.

Char knows me. She knows that she can trust me to keep quiet. Not to squeal. "Yeah, y'all in the clear, as long as you help pay back the cash," I tell her.

Char says she will talk to the twins tomorrow at school. She'll call me later and let me know what they say. Then Char says, "You're my girl, Maleeka. I knew I could count on you."

Dear Diary:

Remember the acorn. Even when you don't see it growing, it's pushing past the dirt. Reaching for the sun. Growing stronger.

—Maleeka

I look at the words on that paper. They sound good all right. But are they true? I don't feel no stronger or braver today than I did a few weeks back. This is stupid, I think, grabbing hold of the page and ripping it out the diary. Then I ball that mess up and throw it in the trash can.

CHAPTER TWENTY-EIGHT

Momma's making me go to sam's store around the corner, even though he ain't never got half the stuff Momma needs or wants. I think she's doing it on purpose, to embarrass me. She just needs some eggs and a slab of bacon for breakfast, she says. Yeah, right.

I tell her I will get Sweets to go with me. Momma says forget about it. She wants only me to go and then come right back home, and not take my own sweet time getting back.

When I go outside, everybody's on their front stoops. Kids, mothers, fathers, cousins. And it seems like everybody's out there to ask me what happened and why a smart girl like me didn't know any better. When I get around the corner and see John-John's face, I know the day can't do nothing but get worse.

"Oooh," he says, strutting across the street like he's cool. "You did it now. They ain't letting you back in school, are they?"

John-John's smiling. He's happy as can be. The worse things are for me, the better some folks like it. John-John's one of those people.

I keep on stepping and counting cracks in the sidewalk while I walk. John-John offers me some gum. No way am I taking anything from him.

"'Least you're keeping your mouth shut," he says, chewing on the gum. "Squealing on your friends ain't even cool."

I stop walking and stare him down. "Ain't nobody to squeal on. I done it by myself."

"You don't have the guts," he says. "They got the right person to pin it on, too. We all know you don't have guts enough to tell."

Me and John-John are walking to the store side by side. I ain't talking, ain't even looking at him. Just walking. Eyes down. Legs pumping. Brain busy thinking about all the mess I'm in. So I don't see some boys coming. They just show up all of a sudden. Crowding in on me and John-John, blocking out the sun with their big selves.

They're after John-John. They say his big mouth got one of them busted for shoplifting. Next thing I know, they're whopping down on John-John. I'm screaming in my head but nothing's coming out of my mouth. John-John's little short arms are stretched out, and his hands are balled up, and he's hitting back as best he can. But there's still three against one. John-John's losing, big time.

Nobody on the street is doing nothing to help him. They're just watching. John-John's already got a busted lip. His left eye is swollen and water, maybe tears, is running out of the right one. I'm standing there shaking my hands and arms like I'm fanning myself dry.

John-John falls to the ground and covers his head with his arms. Those boys are stomping John-John good. Finally, I find my voice. I yell for somebody to call the cops. But folks just stare. I yell some more. Somebody runs inside their house.

Blood. I see blood. John-John, he ain't saying nothing. Ain't moving either. All of a sudden I'm remembering how those other boys messed with me on that day after JuJu's party, and all of a sudden it's like my body's taking orders from somebody else. I'm running across the street, and reaching into some overgrown bushes in front of the house on the corner. I'm pulling and pulling on one of them branches to make me a good switch. I break a few branches loose and run my hand up and down them to get the leaves off. Then I go back to John-John.

One of them boys is looking at me, daring me to use the branches. My heart, it's hurting my chest. Hurting it bad. My hands are burning from yanking and peeling back them leaves. My throat is so dry it's burning too. John-John, he's laying there still getting beat. Next thing I know, I'm hitting them boys. The first boy that I hit yells like a baby. His arm swells up quick. He gets himself off John-John fast and comes for me. I keep swinging. Swinging and sweating and praying for the police to come. I hear their siren getting closer.

Them next two boys are off John-John now, and all of them are coming for me. Coming. I drop that switch and I close my eyes. One boy's got his hands around my arm and squeezing it, the other ones is cursing me good. I'm praying as hard as I can them police get here now. Only I don't hear no siren no more. They gone to somebody else's house, I think. Gone and left me here to die.

Them boys saying they're gonna beat me worse than they beat John-John. I ain't saying nothing. My eyes are closed and pee is about to pour outta me like water. Then I hear some other people talking. Grown-ups. All of a sudden I hear a pop. And a slap. And them boys let me loose and start running. When I open my eyes, they're halfway down the block. And Caleb's standing there. Him and his momma and a whole bunch of grown-ups from the block. It seems like they come right outta thin air.

"Ain't gonna have no girls being beat half to death, not round here," some old man says.

They got brooms and bats and a shovel. Caleb, he's helping John-John up, telling him he can come in his house and get cleaned up. John-John looks a mess, but he's gonna be all right. Caleb's momma asks if I'm OK, if I want to come on inside. "No," I say. I have to go home and let Momma know what happened. I don't say nothing to Caleb. I just give him a weak smile. Me, I'm feeling lucky he came along like he did.

John-John's always talking about how black I am. Well, I'm still the blackest thing in school, and it was me that saved his butt today. People are helping John-John inside Caleb's house, like he's some baby learning to walk. I take myself home.

I don't have to tell Momma much, the story gets to her before I walk in the door. She says she was just about to come for me. She makes me tell her the story three times before she lets me go to my room. After I'm there a while, Momma knocks on my door.

"A letter just came for you. It's from the library. You owe them money?" she asks softly.

I push open the bedroom door before Momma says another word. I snatch the envelope out of her hands.

Dear Ms. Madison:

Congratulations! The third annual Young Writers Committee at the Martin Malcolm Library is pleased to announce you as the winner of this year's contest.

I show Momma the letter. The letter goes on and on about how many people entered, and how they're gonna put my writing on display in the library lobby for a whole month.

I stand there awhile fingering the puffed-up gold letters at the top of the page and reading the letter over and over again.

Momma and me both look at each other. All of a sudden, Momma starts crying. Crying big, fat tears. I don't have to ask her why. I know. We both wishing Daddy was here for the good stuff and the bad.

CHAPTER TWENTY-NINE

Mᴏᴍᴍᴀ ᴡᴇɴᴛ ʀɪɢʜᴛ ᴏᴜᴛ ᴀɴᴅ ʙᴏᴜɢʜᴛ a frame for my congratulations letter. Together we hung the letter up in my room, next to Daddy's poem, which we also put in a frame. I spend the rest of the day trying to figure out what to do about Char.

Maybe I'll call Charlese and tell her I'm sorry, but I gotta tell. Or I'll tell Char that I accidentally told on her. Or I'll tell her the janitor said he saw her. I stomp my feet. Char ain't gonna believe none of that. She's gonna kick my butt if I tell.

You would think after beating those boys off John-John, I wouldn't be afraid of nothing or nobody. But I'm scared like nobody's business. I'm sitting here on the bed rocking. Rocking and sucking my thumb like I did when I was five. Like I do when I get in real trouble and can't figure my way out. I don't have no choice, I gotta tell. Then the phone rings.

"Hi, girlfriend," Charlese says, all sweet. "How you doing?"

At first she makes some small talk about John-John getting beat up. I'm half listening. My hands are shaking. I'm so scared, I almost drop the phone. I take in a long breath and start to tell Char that I'm gonna admit that she made me do everything.

But then Char says, "Me and the twins been talking. We will bring a hundred dollars to your house today. That's the best we can do."

I suck in my breath and say real fast, "I'm sorry I got to do this, Char, but y'all don't leave me no choice. I didn't mess up the classroom by myself so I shouldn't be the only one in trouble and the only one suspended from school. So I'm telling it was your idea and that you made me light that fire. I know you're gonna be mad but that's how it goes, Char."

At first Charlese don't say nothing. She's just breathing. "I knew you'd punk out on me," she says finally. "I knew it."

"I . . . I—"

"Shut up," Char screams. "I'm talking." Then all of a sudden Char starts laughing. Really laughing. The hard kind of laughing that makes your stomach hurt.

"I knew not to trust you. That's why I stole Miss Saunders's watch and slipped it into the slits of your locker," Char says, and busts out laughing again. "And when they searched your locker, guess what?" She laughs. "They found the watch. So they really think you did it now." She laughs for the longest time. "Now tell on me, and I will personally kick your skinny black butt, Maleeka Madison," Char says. "And I won't be by myself, either. You hear me?"

I shake my head yes, like Char can see me. But she knows my answer, because she don't wait around to even hear what it is. Just laughs some more and hangs up the phone.

I walk over to my bed and start rocking. They're expelling me from school. They think I'm a thief and a firebug. I close my eyes and rock some more. I rock till my insides are calm and peaceful.

CHAPTER THIRTY

WHEN I'M FEELING BETTER, I look at the library letter hanging on the wall next to Daddy's poem and the picture of me and him together. I can't even keep the money I won. I have to give it to the school to pay for that mess. Char don't know, and she don't care. All she wants is for me to keep my mouth quiet about her. She's standing over me, getting louder and louder.

Then the doorbell rings. Somebody rings three short, quick times like they're nervous. By the fourth ring, Momma yells for me to get it. She's got her hands full in the kitchen, she says.

When I open the door, Miss Saunders is standing there.

"Maleeka," she says, stretching out her arm and showing me her watch. "You've got some explaining to do."

My eyes get big and my mouth opens wide. Before

Miss Saunders says another word, Momma walks up, holds me close, and tells Miss Saunders to come in.

Momma's talking a lot. She keeps going back and forth between the living room and the kitchen. Tea. Sugar. Homemade biscuits. Honey. It seems like Momma will never sit down. When she finally does, Miss Saunders brings up me and my situation. Right away Momma finds another reason to head to the kitchen.

Miss Saunders talks anyway. "Rumors are going around the school," she says. "Everyone is saying you had help— that it was Charlese's idea to destroy my classroom."

I let her keep talking. I pick at a scab on my hand.

"I'm here to get the truth from you firsthand, to say no matter what, we can work this out, Maleeka."

My eyes shift from Miss Saunders to the floor.

"We need to talk about this, Maleeka."

"Ain't nothing to talk about," I finally say. "I did it. That's that."

"Not alone, you didn't. Everyone knows that. Who helped you?"

"Listen, Miss Saunders. Some kids dared me to do it. Said they'd pay me twenty-five dollars if I did. I needed the money. That's all," I say, digging at the scab, drawing blood from the dry, hard shell.

"Maleeka, once you told me that you could be trusted

to keep a secret. My secret. And you did. I know you did. Now I'm asking *you* to trust *me.*" Miss Saunders turns my way and takes off her jacket. She rolls up the sleeves of her blouse. She reaches her hand out and takes my hand. "Trust me with the truth and I promise everything will be OK," she says softly.

I snatch my hand away. "I said what happened. Why does everybody keep bothering me? Just leave me alone," I say to her.

Miss Saunders sighs and lets my hand drop. She puts her jacket back on and lets herself out.

CHAPTER THIRTY-ONE

I **GO TO SCHOOL THE NEXT DAY.** Miss Saunders has arranged for me to come back. She asks me to meet her in her classroom before school starts. When I arrive, Char is there. Miss Saunders is not wearing a suit. She's got on blue jeans. Miss Saunders is saying something, but I can't make out just what. She and Char are talking at the same time. Char's going on and on about how she didn't have nothing to do with messing up Miss Saunders's room. Miss Saunders is telling me to tell her the whole truth. I want to tell her that the truth will get my butt kicked good. That if I open my big mouth, ain't nothing she or Momma can do to keep Charlese from getting me back. Only I don't say nothing, I just keep my mouth shut.

Charlese looks scared, like she's gonna cry. I never seen that before. I figured that maybe she didn't have no tears.

All the while Char's eyes are saying I better take the blame, or else. I am so tired of being scared, of doing what other folks want me to.

Char throws mean words at me, words as hard as bricks. "You better not punk out on me," she says.

Tears start to roll from my eyes.

"Maleeka. You know what JuJu will do to me if I get kicked out of school."

JuJu will kick Char's butt good. That's another reason why I can't tell. I'm rocking and thinking and crying. Miss Saunders is very quiet. She's listening and watching. She puts a gentle hand on my shoulder.

"If I get in trouble for you, you gonna have to move to another neighborhood," Char is saying.

I keep on rocking and crying.

I'm thinking about the boys who tried to kiss me and the ones I whipped when I helped John-John. I start thinking about Akeelma too.

Now Miss Saunders has her arm around me, and it sure feels good to have her here. She's letting Char speak her mind.

"All I done for you," Char says. "You gonna leave me out to dry like this. Wait till later, you ugly, stupid black thing."

Call me by my name! I hear Akeelma say, and I scream

it out, too. "Call me by my name! I am not ugly. I am not stupid. I am Maleeka Madison, and, yeah, I'm black, real black, and if you don't like me, too bad 'cause black is the skin I'm in!" I yell. "No matter what you think, Charlese Jones, you're ten times worse. I would never force someone to burn down a classroom, or pick on kids weaker than me, or say words so mean they make people bleed inside." I'm rocking and crying and rocking. "You the one who pushed me to mess up Miss Saunders's room, and you were in on it, too—you and the twins," I say, feeling relieved.

Charlese gives me a hard look.

She pushes past Miss Saunders and me and makes her way to the door. "Look at you two—two ugly-faced losers," she says. Miss Saunders don't even stop Char. She lets her go. Then Miss Saunders hugs me to her, and I feel safe inside.

CHAPTER THIRTY-TWO

A WEEK PASSES. Raina and Raise have been suspended, and nobody's seen Char. When the twins return, they tell everybody that JuJu sent Char to live with her grandparents in Alabama. Kids are still saying how jive I am for squealing on Char. But I don't care. Char can't hurt me now.

Mr. Pajolli says my office job is over, that I've paid enough dues by telling the truth about Char. I hunch my shoulders up like I don't care about the office, but deep down inside I feel kind of bad. I was starting to really like it. And I missed working there when I was suspended. As I'm leaving the office, Caleb is standing by my locker. He turns all red when I ask what he's doing.

"I was just leaving," he says, handing me a purple letter with gold writing on it. "Wait till I'm gone before you open it, all right?"

I nod, and watch him go to class. I duck into the girls' room, drop the backpack on the floor, and open the letter real slow. Spearmint. It smells like spearmint gum. I take the gum out and put it in my mouth before I read the letter. It's a poem. For me.

To Maleeka: My sweet dark chocolate candy girl

Would you be my Almond Joy
My chocolate chip, my Hershey Kiss
My sweet dark chocolate butter crisp?

Hand and hand we'd walk to class
and sit and talk in sweet green grass.

Rollar coaster way up high,
pick moonbeams from out the sky.

Would you be my Almond Joy
My chocolate chip, my Hershey Kiss
My sweet dark chocolate butter crisp?

Caleb's poem makes me cry. It is so sweet. I look at my face in the mirror and smile. I promise myself to hang

Caleb's poem on the wall with Daddy's and the one from the library.

On the way to class, I see Caleb. He is still red-faced. Even his ears are red. My heart is beating fast, but I go up to him anyway. "That is the nicest thing anybody ever did for me," I say, with this goofy smile on my face. And we stand there, me twisting a pencil in my hands and him twisting one of his braids over and over again.

"You two supposed to be somewhere?" Mr. Braxton, the gym teacher, asks.

"Yeah," we both say.

"I'm going to Miss Saunders's class," I say.

"And I'm on my way to math class," says Caleb.

"Well, get there—now." Mr. Braxton's pointing.

"I'll walk you to Miss Saunders's room. It's on my way," Caleb says, still twisting his hair.

I take his letter and put it in my backpack, and we walk down the hall together. I close my eyes for a second, and take a deep breath. Caleb always smells so fresh and clean. That's another thing I like about him.

When I finally walk into class, everybody's staring at me like I got two heads. I'm late, but Miss Saunders doesn't make an issue of it today.

Class is in the detention room, while Miss Saunders's room is being repaired. Miss Saunders is giving us twenty pages of *Ali Baba and the Forty Thieves* to read by tomorrow and telling us she's been easy on us so far, but things are about to heat up.

"Welcome back, Miss Madison," Miss Saunders says, giving me a wink. "Class wouldn't be the same unless you were late."

Everybody laughs and turns my way. "Yeah," John-John says, "welcome back."

ACKNOWLEDGMENTS

Special thanks to
Grampa Titus and Poppop
(James "Jimmy Sax" Rosseau),
who had the talent but not the opportunity,
Mom, Dad, Gramma Marie, Uncle Jimmy,
Aunt Betty, and Uncle Sam,
who always knew how to tell a good story.
Thanks, too, to August Wilson and his sister
Freda Ellis, to Highlights for Children, Rob Penny,
Joy Cowley, and Ed and Helen Palascak and the kids.

Turn the page for a sneak peek at

BANG!

BY **SHARON G. FLAKE**

CHAPTER ONE

THEY KILL PEOPLE where I live. They shoot 'em dead for no real reason. You don't duck, you die. That's what happened to my brother Jason. He was seven. Playing on our front porch. Laughing. Then some man ran by yelling, "He gonna kill me. He's gonna—"

Before the man finished saying what he had to say, a boy no older than me chased him up our front porch steps. The man yelled for Jason to get out the way. But Jason just stood there crying. Right then, the boy pulls out a gun and starts shooting.

Bang! Guns really sound like that, you know. *Bang!* And people bleed from everywhere and blood is redder than you think. *Bang!* And little kids look funny in caskets. That's 'cause they ain't meant to be in one, I guess.

My brother died two years ago. But I can't stop thinking about him. And I can't walk in the house through the front door no more because of the blood. My mother says it's gone. "See?" she says, pointing to the porch floor and the gray wooden chairs. "Long gone." But I can still see it. I can. So I come into the house through the back way. Stepping over the missing stoop Jason used to put his green plastic soldiers in. Opening the iron gate that my dad put up to keep trouble out. Going inside the house and not looking at my brother's room, because if I even see his door, I cry. And a thirteen-year-old boy ain't supposed to cry, is he?

The day Jason died I was with Journey—a horse. She stays at Dream-a-Lot Stables, not far from where I live. It's a broke-down stable where kids hit her with rocks and try to make her eat sticks. But my father, he taught me and Jason to ride Journey, and brush her good. So even though she ain't ours, Journey likes us best. The man who owns the stables and rents out broke-down horses for five bucks an hour would let us ride for almost free, long as we cleaned Journey's stable first. So that morning, after my mom and dad went to work, I left Jason home by hisself. I walked to the stables and brushed the flies and dirt off Journey's blond coat. I swept up turds as big as turtles, and rode Journey all the way home—up the avenue and past Seventh Street, between honking cars, slow buses, and grown-ups who patted her butt, then got mad when she broke wind in their faces.

When I got home, Jason was on the porch. He asked me to play toy soldiers with him. I wouldn't. Journey was thirsty. So I went around back to get a hose so she could drink. That's when I heard the man yelling, and Jason screaming my name. I ran to the front of the house. The boy chased the man up our steps and onto our porch. Journey shook her head and stomped her feet on the pavement. The gun went off. The hose in my hand soaked the porch, squirted the dead man and splashed blood everywhere. Neighbors tried to pull it away from me, but I wouldn't turn it loose. That's what they say anyhow.

After Jason was gone, I saw a psychologist for six months. But my father didn't like that, so I quit going. "You a man, not no sissy baby girl," he said when he found me one day behind the couch, crying.

My mother got mad at him. "I'm gonna cry over my baby boy till I die," she said, hugging me. "Guess Mann here's gonna cry awhile too."

My father used to be in the army, so he don't cry

much. And he don't want no boy crying all the time neither. That's what he tells me anyhow.

A week ago my mother told my father I needed help. "We all do," she said, sitting down on the living-room floor next to me. "It's been nearly two years since Jason died, and it hurts like it happened this morning."

My father stood behind his favorite brown leather chair. "I don't need no help. And him," he said, pointing to me, "ain't nothing that momma's boy needs but a good old-fashioned butt-kicking."

I am not a momma's boy, but since Jason died, that's what my dad calls me. "People die," he said. "Little people die too. Get over it."

My mother jumped up. Her knee knocked me in the chin. I held my mouth, because I bit my tongue and I didn't want her feeling bad about that. "So you're over it, huh?" she said, running up to the window and pulling back the white curtains. "Yeah, right," she said, holding on to the heavy, iron bars that cover every window and door in our house.

My mother walked past my father and unlocked the drawer to his desk. She picked up his .38 and stuck her arm high in the air like she does when she's hailing a cab. Then she reached in the drawer with her other hand and pulled out a rusty hunting knife big enough to cut your arm off. "He cries," she said, looking at me and pointing the gun at my father, "but you, you—"

"Shut up, Grace. I'm warning you."

My mother kept talking. Next thing I knew my father was pulling his gun and knife out her hands and locking them back in the drawer. She hugged him from behind. "He didn't deserve to die. He was sweet and smart and gave hugs when you—"

My dad covered his ears with his hands. *"Grace!"*

She ran to the window and yelled out. "You killed us too! We look like we still alive but we dead. Rotten inside." She punched her flat stomach. Bit down on her arm. "Ja . . . Ja . . ."

My father shook her. "Don't say his name! Don't ever—"

My mother's eyes are big red circles with black bags under 'em that won't go away since Jason died. "He's gonna be nine in a few months," she said. "We have to make a cake. Buy him something special."

My dad spit at the trash can. Some made it in. The rest stuck to the outside like a slug. "A dead boy don't need no presents. I told you that last year."

We always get cakes on our birthdays. And we

always sing songs and make the day extra special, not just for me and Jason, but for my mom and dad too. My mother says it wouldn't be right to leave Jason out now. So she gets him presents he can't open and makes him cakes he can't eat.

My dad said what my mother never wants to hear. "Grace. He's gone. And he ain't never coming back."

I watched her, 'cause I knew them words were gonna get her too sad to make supper, or laugh when the funny shows came on TV tonight.

My mother went to the front door and opened it wide. Then she ran onto the porch and yelled for Jason. My dad ran after her. But by the time he got there, she was on her knees picking up little green soldiers we find on the porch sometimes but can't figure out just how they get there. She stomped her feet. "Jason. You come home. Come home right now!"

My father kneeled down beside her. He rubbed her lips, then covered up the rest of her words with his fingers. And then he cried, right along with her.

CHAPTER TWO

THREE DAYS LATER my father apologized. He said he was sorry for making my mother so upset. Sorry for saying all them things about Jason. She was glad he said it. After that, they got dressed and went to the movies. I went to my room and tried to figure out why she couldn't figure out that tomorrow he was gonna say them same things all over again.

"He can't help it," she says all the time. "He just doesn't know what to do with all the things he's feeling inside."

I know she's right. Only I get tired of him being mean. He used to be different. He used to take us to the park. Slide down snow hills with us and lie in bed between me and Jason and make up stories about two boys walking from here to China. Then Jason died and so did my dad, kinda.

One time, when my mother and him were arguing about the way he treated me, she made me go get some of Jason's things. I walked over to the middle bookshelf and picked up Jason's lunch box—the one he had in his hand that day he got killed.

"Give it here," my mother said. She opened it. Took out the note. "'Daddy loves you.'"

My father snatched the napkin out her hand and tore it up.

My mother pointed to a Buster Brown shoe box sitting way on top of the bookshelf. "I still got the rest," she said, talking about the other notes my dad had put in Jason's lunch box. *Have a nice day,* they'd say. *Meet me after school for coffee,* he'd write. Only he never gave Jason real coffee—just grape juice in a coffee mug. "Us men have to have something strong now and then," he'd say. That always made Jason laugh.

I got notes every day too, when I was Jason's age. But when I turned nine, they stopped. My father took me to the yard right after my birthday party that year, and burned them. "What's between a father and his son," he said, putting one hand on his heart and the other on mine, "can't be burned by fire, washed away by water, or destroyed with human hands." He squeezed me so hard, I couldn't breathe. Then he gave me a note—the same note he gives me every year on my birthday. *What we have is forever* it says. When I was ten, I got to hold on to the note for ten hours. At thirteen, I kept it for thirteen hours. When my time's up, I give it back to him until my next birthday. I always liked getting that note. But I don't believe it no more.

Praise for SHARON G. FLAKE

THE SKIN I'M IN

Winner of the Coretta Scott King / John Steptoe
Award for New Talent

New York Public Library Top Ten Books
for the Teen Age

★ "Flake's debut novel will hit home."
—*Publishers Weekly* (starred review)

BANG!

ALA Best Books for Young Adults

VOYA Top Shelf Fiction

"Disturbing, thought-provoking."
—*School Library Journal*

WHO AM I WITHOUT HIM?

Coretta Scott King Author Honor Book

★ "Honest and valuable."
—*Kirkus Reviews* (starred review)

★ "Hilarious and anguished, these twelve
short stories . . . speak with rare truth."
—*Booklist* (starred review)

YOU DON'T EVEN KNOW ME
The companion to *Who Am I Without Him?*

"These complex and thought-provoking stories
won't disappoint."
—*School Library Journal*

"The immediate voices . . . are well-suited for
readers' theater and for sharing everywhere."
—*Booklist*

MONEY HUNGRY
Coretta Scott King Author Honor Book

Los Angeles Times Recommended Book for Teens

★ "Razor-sharp dialogue . . . a story that's
immediate, vivid, and unsensationalized."
—*Booklist* (starred review)

BEGGING FOR CHANGE
The sequel to *Money Hungry*

An ALA Quick Pick

A *Bulletin* Blue Ribbon Book

★ "Flake's charged, infectious dialogue will sweep
readers through the first-person story . . . Hopeful."
—*Booklist* (starred review)

Sharon G. Flake's breakout novel, *The Skin I'm In*, established her as a favorite among middle and high school students, parents, and educators worldwide. She has spoken to more than two hundred thousand young people, and hugged nearly as many. Her work—nine novels, numerous short stories, plays, and a picture book entitled *You Are Not a Cat*—has been translated into multiple languages, including French, Korean, and Portuguese. She is the recipient of numerous awards, such as the Coretta Scott King Honor and the YWCA Racial Justice Award, and her books have been named to many prestigious lists, including *Kirkus Review*'s Top Ten Books of the Year, Best Books for Young Adults by the American Library Association, Top Ten Books for the Teen Age by the New York Public Library, Top Twenty Recommended Books to Read by the Texas Library Association, and *Booklist* Editor's Choice, among others. She lives in Pittsburgh, Pennsylvania. For more information, go to sharongflake.com, or follow her on Twitter @sharonflake.